# Sherlock Holmes and The Haunted Museum

Mabel Swift

Copyright © 2024 by Mabel Swift

www.mabelswift.com

All rights reserved.

No portion of this book may be reproduced in any form without written permission from the publisher or author.

# Contents

| | |
|---|---|
| Chapter 1 | 1 |
| Chapter 2 | 9 |
| Chapter 3 | 19 |
| Chapter 4 | 25 |
| Chapter 5 | 31 |
| Chapter 6 | 38 |
| Chapter 7 | 45 |
| Chapter 8 | 53 |
| Chapter 9 | 61 |
| Chapter 10 | 69 |
| Chapter 11 | 77 |
| Chapter 12 | 85 |
| Chapter 13 | 90 |
| Chapter 14 | 98 |

| | |
|---|---|
| Chapter 15 | 106 |
| Chapter 16 | 115 |
| Chapter 17 | 120 |
| Chapter 18 | 127 |
| Chapter 19 | 133 |
| Chapter 20 | 142 |
| Chapter 21 | 146 |
| Chapter 22 | 153 |
| Chapter 23 | 160 |
| Chapter 24 | 166 |
| Chapter 25 | 177 |
| A note from the author | 179 |

# Chapter 1

Sherlock Holmes gazed pensively out of the window of his Baker Street lodgings, his keen, grey eyes surveying the bustling London street below. His brilliant mind, ever active and hungry for stimulation, pondered the next perplexing case that would inevitably find its way to his doorstep. Dr Watson, his stalwart companion and chronicler of their many adventures together, sat in his customary armchair by the crackling fire, the morning paper spread across his lap as he perused the day's news with a thoughtful expression.

"I say, Holmes," Watson remarked. "Listen to this peculiar headline: 'Ghostly Activities at Waxworks Museum.' Apparently, there have been numerous reports of strange and inexplicable occurrences at that museum of wax figures not far from here. You know the one; it opened about a year ago, I think."

"I know the one," Holmes replied without turning around. "Although, I haven't visited the place as yet. Perhaps I'll get around to it soon."

Watson said, "Would you like me to read this article out loud? About the strange occurrences that are happening? Some visitors claim the museum is haunted."

Holmes held up his hand. "You can stop there, Watson. I have no interest in such sensational claims. There is always a rational explanation for such so-called hauntings and supernatural activities. We have proved this many times using the power of logic and deduction."

Watson chuckled, folding the paper neatly and setting it aside on the side table. "Right, you are, Holmes. I'll read it later. No doubt the famous medium, Madam Rosalind, will make a grand appearance at the museum to commune with the alleged spirits that haunt its rooms. Doesn't she always appear at such times as these?"

At the mere mention of the medium's name, Holmes's face darkened. "She does, and with more regularity than I care for. Whenever there are claims of ghostly goings-on, Madam Rosalind is never far behind, offering her services. I would be quite content to never cross paths with that infernal woman again. Her constant attempts to offer her so-called psychic services whenever we take on a new case are most unwelcome and distracting. She has a calculating look in her eyes. One I've seen in hardened criminals. There's something untrustworthy about that woman."

With a smile, Watson said, "There will be no more talk of Madam Rosalind and her calculating eyes."

Holmes continued to gaze out of the window. His eyes narrowed as he studied the passersby. "I wonder when our next case will present itself. It feels like an eternity since we last had a mystery to unravel."

Watson replied, "It's only been a week since we concluded the affair of the missing crown. Surely you can't be growing restless already?"

"Ah, but you know me," Holmes replied. "My mind rebels at stagnation. Give me problems, give me work, give me the most puzzling mystery possible, I am in my proper atmosphere. But this inactivity is something I cannot abide."

Rising from his armchair, Watson joined his friend at the window, his eyes following Holmes's gaze to the bustling street below. "Perhaps there are new mysteries to be found right here, amongst the ordinary lives of London's citizens."

Holmes's eyes sparkled with interest. "Indeed, Watson. Take, for example, that young woman hurrying along with a bundle clutched tightly to her chest. What secrets might she be carrying?"

Watson studied the woman in question, taking note of her furtive looks and how she seemed to shrink away from the other pedestrians. "Perhaps she's fleeing from an unhappy marriage, or maybe she's stolen something valuable and fears being caught."

"Very possible," Holmes said, his attention already shifting to another figure on the street. "And what about that elderly gentleman, walking with a pronounced limp and a faraway look in his eyes?"

"A war veteran, I'd wager," Watson replied, his own military background allowing him to recognise the tell tale signs. "Haunted by the memories of battles long past, and perhaps nursing a wound that never fully healed."

Holmes nodded, a hint of admiration in his voice. "Your medical expertise serves you well, my dear friend."

As they continued to observe the passersby, Holmes's keen eyes alighted upon a young man who seemed to be in a great hurry, his face pale and his hands trembling. "Now, Watson, what do you make of that fellow?"

Watson furrowed his brow, studying the man intently. "He appears to be in a state of great agitation, Holmes.

Perhaps he's just received some terrible news, or maybe he's fleeing from some sort of trouble."

"Ah, but look closer, Watson," Holmes urged. "Notice the ink stains on his fingers, the slight bulge in his coat pocket that suggests a small notebook, and the way he glances left and right, as if searching for someone or something."

"A journalist, then?" Watson ventured, beginning to see the clues that Holmes had so easily discerned.

"Precisely, Watson. And not just any journalist, but one who has stumbled upon a story of great importance. The question is, what could have made him so unsettled?"

His tone deliberately solemn, Watson suggested, "Is it possible there's been a development in that perplexing haunting at the museum? Maybe our dear acquaintance, Madam Rosalind, is due to pay a visit there at any moment and despatch any impish phantoms. And our young journalist out there doesn't want to miss a second of this latest development."

Holmes let out a loud laugh that startled Watson. "You could very well be correct! I've half a mind to run after that fellow and see where he is going."

"Even if it leads to Madam Rosalind?" Watson jested.

"Ah, you have a point. We'll leave the fellow alone." He looked left and right. "Now, who else do we spy out there?"

As they continued to observe the street below, a particular figure caught Holmes' eye. A man, dressed in a fashionable hat and an expensive-looking overcoat, was pacing back and forth in front of their building, his movements erratic and hesitant.

"Watson," Holmes said, "do you see that man down there? The one in the hat and overcoat?"

Watson leaned closer to the window, squinting to get a better look. "Yes, I see him. He seems rather agitated, doesn't he?"

"He does," Holmes agreed, his attention never leaving the man. "His behaviour is most peculiar. It's as if he's wrestling with some internal dilemma, unsure of whether to approach our door or not."

They watched as the man took a few determined steps towards the entrance of 221B Baker Street, only to abruptly turn away at the last moment. He walked a short distance, then paused, his shoulders slumping as if in defeat.

"He's changed his mind," Watson observed. "But why? What could be troubling him so?"

Holmes replied, "I suspect we may have a potential client on our hands. A man who is grappling with a problem so perplexing, so overwhelming, that he fears to even seek our assistance. Notice the way he keeps glancing at our windows, the tension in his shoulders. There is something troubling him. Something he needs to share with another person."

As if on cue, the man turned around once more, his steps now filled with a newfound determination as he approached the door of 221B Baker Street. Holmes and Watson watched as he raised his hand, hesitating for the briefest of moments before finally knocking.

The sound echoed through the house, a sharp and insistent rap that seemed to hang in the air. Moments later, the door was opened and Mrs Hudson's muffled voice could be heard as she greeted the visitor.

"Well, Watson," Holmes said, a glint of excitement in his eyes, "it appears our lull in activity is about to come to an end. Shall we see what mystery this gentleman brings to our doorstep?"

Holmes dashed to his chair, urging Watson to do the same, insisting they must be seated before their guest's arrival, lest he suspect they had been peering at him through the window.

Watson looked as if he might say that they had been doing exactly that, but thought better of it and instead hurried to his own chair, swiftly arranging himself in a posture of studied indifference.

They waited as Mrs Hudson's footsteps grew louder, accompanied by the heavier tread of their mysterious visitor. The door to their sitting room opened.

# Chapter 2

Mrs Hudson entered the sitting room, followed closely by the visitor. "Gentlemen," she said, "this is Mr Alfred Chamberlain. He's here to see you about a matter of some urgency."

The man took off his hat and overcoat and gave them to Mrs Hudson, who already had her hands extended towards him.

Holmes rose from his chair, extending his hand in greeting. "Mr Chamberlain, welcome. I am Sherlock Holmes, and this is my colleague, Dr John Watson. Please, come in and have a seat."

Mr Chamberlain was a portly man in his late fifties. He had bushy eyebrows and a jovial face, and was dressed in a tailored suit that strained slightly at the buttons. His handshake was firm. "Pleased to meet you, both of you."

Mrs Hudson turned to Holmes. "Shall I bring up some refreshments, Mr Holmes?"

"Yes, thank you, Mrs Hudson. That would be most appreciated," Holmes replied with a nod.

Mrs Hudson left the room, closing the door behind her. Chamberlain was invited to take a seat. A light sheen of perspiration lay upon his brow.

"Now, Mr Chamberlain," Holmes began, settling back into his own chair, "what brings you to our doorstep today? I can see that you are troubled by something."

Chamberlain cleared his throat, his glance darting between Holmes and Watson. "Well, Mr Holmes, it's a bit of a delicate matter. I'm not quite sure how to begin."

Holmes said, "Mr Chamberlain, I assure you that no problem is ever too delicate for our assistance. Please, feel free to speak freely."

Chamberlain nodded, taking a deep breath. "You see, gentlemen, I am the proprietor of a waxworks museum. It opened over a year ago, and we've been doing quite well. That is, until recently."

Watson, who had been listening intently, suddenly sat up straighter. "I say, Mr Chamberlain, your museum wouldn't happen to be the one mentioned in this morning's paper, would it? The one with the alleged ghostly activity?"

He held up the newspaper, the headline clearly visible. Chamberlain's face reddened, and he shifted uncomfortably in his seat.

"Yes, Dr Watson, I'm afraid that is indeed my establishment. I don't know how the press got news of it. But I must stress that I do not believe in the supernatural whatsoever. There must be a logical explanation for the strange occurrences."

Holmes' eyes lit up with interest. "Ah, I am glad to hear that your views on the supernatural match my own. I'm eager to learn more of these strange occurrences you speak of. Please, Mr Chamberlain, do go on."

Chamberlain settled back in his chair. "It started recently. Small things at first. Objects moving on their own, strange noises suddenly filling the air, ghostly figures moving through the corridors. But then it escalated."

"I see," Holmes said. "Please, continue."

Chamberlain paused, as if steeling himself for what he was about to say next. "One of our most popular exhibits, a wax figure of William Shakespeare, had disappeared, leaving only his quill behind. He turned up later, standing next to Captain Blackbeard. The two figures had been turned towards each other as if in cahoots. You should have heard the complaints we received about that, especially from a local historian who had decided to visit us that day. And then, just two days later, a figure of Jack the Ripper vanished entirely from its usual position, only to reappear in a different part of the museum which was created for our younger visitors. Some of the smallest children erupted into tears when they saw the menacing look on Jack's face. Oh! The complaints I received from furious parents that day!"

Watson's eyes widened. "Good heavens!"

Holmes, however, remained impassive. "Forgive me for asking, Mr Chamberlain, but are these merely pranks or publicity stunts? I'm not saying they were committed by you, but maybe someone you employ?"

Chamberlain shook his head vehemently. "The people I employ would never stoop to such a thing. I trust them implicitly, no doubt about that. What troubles me, is how the newspapers have labelled this as ghostly activity. That isn't good for my business and visitor numbers are already falling. I know there must be a reasonable explanation behind these strange events, but I'm at a loss to think what that could be."

At that moment, Mrs Hudson returned with a tray of tea and biscuits. She set it down on the table, casting a curious glance at Chamberlain before leaving the room once more.

As Holmes poured the tea, he said, "Mr Chamberlain, I am pleased to hear that you seek a logical explanation for the strange occurrences at your museum. From the details I have so far, I suspect a human hand is behind these, and not that of a spectral nature."

He handed a cup to Chamberlain, who accepted it with a grateful nod. "Thank you, Mr Holmes. I knew coming to you was the right decision, even though it took some courage to knock on your door, considering the nature of my problem. I was so embarrassed at the prospect of asking you to look into my supposed haunted museum. Will you help me get to the bottom of this mystery?"

Holmes smiled. "My dear Mr Chamberlain, nothing would give me greater pleasure. Dr Watson and I will be happy to lend our assistance."

Watson, who had been helping himself to a biscuit, looked up in surprise. "We will?"

Holmes shot him a smile. "Of course we will, Watson. A case like this, where we get to debunk supernatural rumours, is just the sort of challenge I relish." He turned back to Chamberlain. "Now, Mr Chamberlain, please tell us everything you know about these activities. Leave out no detail, no matter how insignificant it may seem."

Chamberlain, looking visibly relieved, began to recount his tale in earnest. "It all started about three weeks ago," he said. "A young lady, quite distressed, came rushing to me, claiming that one of the waxworks in an exhibit room had moved."

Holmes said, "Moved, you say? In what manner?"

"She said it had shifted slightly to the left, right before her eyes. The poor girl was convinced it had come to life. She let out a scream that echoed through the entire museum. She ran out of the exhibit room in a state of sheer terror. It was that scream that made me run towards her. She looked as if she was about to faint."

Watson's eyebrows rose in surprise. "That must have been quite a shock for her."

Chamberlain nodded, his expression grim. "At the time, I tried to reassure her, suggesting that perhaps a sudden, strong gust of wind had caused the movement. After all, these things do happen in old buildings like ours."

Holmes, however, seemed unconvinced. "A gust of wind? Was the waxwork figure in an enclosed exhibit room or near a doorway?"

Chamberlain shifted uncomfortably in his seat. "It was in an enclosed room, and, well, it was the only explanation I could think of at the moment. I didn't want to alarm the young lady further."

"Understandable," Holmes said, his tone neutral. "Please, do go on."

"I thought nothing more of it," Chamberlain continued, "until I started receiving other complaints. More visitors claimed to have seen the waxworks moving, and then there were the sounds..."

"Sounds?" Watson asked.

"Yes, Dr Watson. Eerie noises, coming from all directions. Whispers, creaks, and even the occasional moan. It was as if the museum itself had come alive."

Holmes asked, "And when did these sounds begin?"

"A few days after the first incident with the young lady," Chamberlain replied. "It wasn't long before rumours started circulating that the museum was haunted. Visitor numbers began to fall, and then the newspaper got wind of the story and those rumours have increased tenfold."

"I can well imagine," Holmes said in understanding.

Chamberlain continued, "Mr Holmes, if these rumours persist, I fear my museum will be forced to close its doors. I simply cannot afford to lose any more business."

Holmes nodded, his expression one of deep thought. "I understand your concerns, Mr Chamberlain. Now, do you have any suspects in mind? Someone who would like to see the closing of your museum?"

Chamberlain looked up, his eyes wide. "Yes, Mr Holmes. There is someone who I believe would like to see my museum fail and take great joy in it."

"And who might that be?" Holmes asked.

Chamberlain said, "Marcus Bramwell. He's my ex-business partner. I'm almost certain he's the one behind this."

"What makes you suspect him?" Holmes asked.

Chamberlain sighed. "We had a falling out three years ago over a financial matter. I'd rather not go into the details, but suffice it to say, it was a messy affair. Bramwell has been out for revenge ever since."

Watson frowned. "Revenge is a powerful motive. Has he made any direct threats?"

"Not directly, no," Chamberlain admitted. "But I wouldn't put it past him to employ people to sabotage the museum on his behalf. He's a cunning man, and he knows how to cover his tracks."

Holmes nodded. "Interesting. And where might we find this Marcus Bramwell?"

Chamberlain said, "He's set up a rival tourist attraction, Bramwell's Hall of Scientific Marvels. It's probably receiving all the tourists who no longer visit the waxworks museum."

Holmes said, "Bramwell's Hall of Scientific Marvels? I've heard of it. It's been gaining quite a reputation of late."

"Yes, it has," Chamberlain said, his tone bitter. "While my museum struggles, his thrives. It's as if he's stealing my customers right from under my nose."

Watson looked at Holmes. "What do you think, Holmes? Could Bramwell be behind these disturbances?"

Holmes tapped his chin, deep in thought. "It's certainly a possibility, Watson. A man with a grudge and a rival business. It's a classic motive. Mr Chamberlain, Dr Watson and I will pay a visit to your ex-business partner and see what he has to say for himself. After that, I would like to visit your museum, to examine the scene of these disturbances firsthand."

Chamberlain nodded eagerly. "Of course, Mr Holmes. I'll give you a personal tour. When would be convenient for you?"

Holmes glanced at the clock on the mantelpiece. "Shall we say, three o'clock this afternoon? That should give us ample time to speak with Mr Bramwell and then make our way to your establishment."

"Three o'clock it is," Chamberlain agreed, rising from his seat. "Thank you, Mr Holmes, Dr Watson. I can't tell you how much I appreciate your help."

Holmes also stood, shaking Chamberlain's hand. "We'll do our best to get to the bottom of this mystery, Mr Chamberlain. You have my word."

With that, Chamberlain took his leave, the relief on his face palpable. As the door closed behind him, Watson turned to Holmes.

"Well, Holmes, what do you make of it all?" he asked.

Holmes picked up his pipe, turning it over in his hands. "It's a curious case, Watson. There is much to unravel here, one of them the intriguing matter of the financial dispute between the two businessmen. I would like to find out what happened there. It could be related to what's occurring at the museum now. Let's speak with Marcus Bramwell and see what he has to say."

Watson nodded, reaching for his hat and coat. "Then let's be off, Holmes. The game, as they say, is afoot."

Holmes laughed. "Indeed, it is, Watson. Indeed, it is."

# Chapter 3

Holmes and Watson hailed a hansom cab and made their way to Bramwell's Hall of Scientific Marvels. As they approached the building, they couldn't help but be impressed by its modern design. The clean lines and large, plate-glass windows stood in stark contrast to the gothic architecture of the surrounding buildings. Electric lights framed the entrance, beckoning visitors to come and witness the marvels of technology within.

After paying for their tickets, they entered the impressive building and found themselves in a sleek and utilitarian interior, designed to showcase the exhibits rather than the architecture itself. The main hall was filled with interactive displays and machines, each demonstrating the latest technological advancements of the era. A working model of a steam engine caught Watson's eye, while Holmes was drawn to the early electrical devices on display.

It was clear that Bramwell's attraction appealed to the public's fascination with science and innovation, offering a glimpse into the future that was both exciting and awe-inspiring.

As they were examining a particularly intricate display, a tall and distinguished figure approached them. With his neatly trimmed beard and penetrating blue eyes, the man exuded confidence and intelligence. His salt and pepper hair lent him an air of distinguished maturity, while his impeccably tailored dark suit spoke of his success and status.

"Ah, Mr Sherlock Holmes and Dr John Watson, I presume?" the man said, his voice smooth and charming. "I am Marcus Bramwell. I saw you through the window of my office and recognised you immediately from photographs that have appeared in the newspapers. May I ask, is your visit one of pleasure or of business?"

Holmes said, "Our visit is of a business nature, Mr Bramwell. We were hoping to have a word with you regarding a matter of some importance."

Bramwell smiled, but there was a coldness behind it. "Of course, gentlemen. Please, follow me to my office, where we can speak more privately."

As they followed Bramwell to his office, Holmes noticed the approving looks the man received from several women they passed. It was clear that Bramwell's charm and enigmatic nature made him a favourite among the fairer sex.

Once they were seated in Bramwell's office, the man leaned back in his chair. "So, gentlemen, what brings you to my humble establishment?"

Holmes explained, "We're here on behalf of Mr Alfred Chamberlain, the owner of the waxwork museum across town."

Bramwell's smile tightened almost imperceptibly. "Ah, yes. Poor Alfred. I heard he's been having some trouble lately."

Holmes continued, "He believes that someone may be deliberately sabotaging his business. As a result, his visitor numbers have dwindled."

Bramwell raised an eyebrow. "And he thinks the person responsible for the sabotage is me?"

Holmes didn't answer immediately, instead studying Bramwell's reaction. After a moment, he said, "He mentioned that you two had a falling out some years ago."

Bramwell waved a hand dismissively. "A minor disagreement, nothing more. Certainly nothing that would drive me to sabotage his business."

Watson spoke, his tone curious. "Mr Bramwell, is it possible that your establishment has benefited from the misfortunes of Mr Chamberlain's museum?"

Bramwell's eyes flashed, but his voice remained calm. "Dr Watson, success in business is often a matter of seizing opportunities when they arise. If Alfred's misfortune has driven more customers to my doors, well, that's simply the nature of competition. Was there anything else? I've got a busy day ahead of me."

Holmes said, "Mr Bramwell, would you like to know the specific acts of sabotage that have taken place at Mr Chamberlain's establishment? Aren't you the least bit curious?"

Bramwell retrieved a folded newspaper from the side of his desk, a knowing smile on his face. "I'm already aware of what's happened, at least according to the press." He tapped the newspaper with his finger.

"And what do you make of the gossip that the troubles are of a supernatural nature?" Holmes asked.

Bramwell scoffed, his eyes narrowing. "Not likely. I don't believe in any of that nonsense."

Watson asked, "Do you have any theories about what might be behind these incidents, Mr Bramwell?"

Bramwell answered, "It could be an insider job."

Holmes raised an eyebrow. "Mr Chamberlain assured us that his staff are loyal."

A cold smile spread across Bramwell's face. "That isn't the case with some of them. I suggest you talk to the staff more closely, especially one of the sculptors who has been overheard in a public house complaining about how he's been treated by Mr Chamberlain."

"And do you have a name for this disgruntled sculptor?" Holmes asked.

Bramwell shrugged. "I've no idea. Isn't it your job to find that out, Mr Holmes? You are a detective, after all."

Holmes stood, buttoning his jacket, not appreciating the mockery in Bramwell's voice. "Thank you for your time and the information you've provided. It has been most enlightening."

Watson stood as well, nodding to Bramwell. "Yes, thank you, Mr Bramwell."

As they left Bramwell's office and walked away, Holmes turned to Watson, his brow furrowed in thought. "I believe there's more to this than meets the eye. Bramwell's demeanour and his readiness to point the finger at Chamberlain's staff raises some interesting questions."

Watson nodded. "You think he might have ulterior motives?"

"It's a possibility we can't ignore," Holmes said, his pace quickening as they exited the Hall of Scientific Marvels. "We need to speak with Chamberlain's staff, particularly this sculptor Bramwell mentioned. But we must also keep an open mind. There could be other factors at play here."

They hailed a cab and asked the driver to take them to Mr Chamberlain's Waxwork Museum. As they settled in their seats, Holmes' mind was already filling with questions and theories. He was determined to solve the mystery as soon as possible.

# Chapter 4

A short while later, Holmes and Watson approached the imposing façade of Chamberlain's Waxwork Museum. Holmes sensed there was an air of unease hanging over the building. A small queue had formed at the entrance, and as they took their place in line, snippets of worried conversation reached their ears.

"I heard it's haunted," whispered a young woman to her companion. "People say there are restless spirits roaming around the displays. And there are strange sounds like the dead calling out for help."

Her friend nodded, glancing nervously at the museum's darkened windows. "They say the wax figures come to life at night and walk around. I hope they don't come to life when we're inside. I can't be doing with anything spooky. If we see anything like that, I'll leave and I won't be coming back, I can tell you."

Holmes and Watson exchanged a knowing look but didn't say anything.

They soon reached the ticket booth.

Holmes stepped forward, offering the woman behind the counter a charming smile. "Good morning, madam," he greeted, his tone warm and friendly. "We would love to visit this fine establishment, but I have to say, I overheard some rather intriguing rumours about this place whilst waiting in line. Is it true the museum is haunted?"

The woman's face, already lined with worry, seemed to fall even further at Holmes' question. She shook her head, her voice strained as she replied, "No, sir, it isn't. I've been told to inform any patrons that if they have complaints about their visit, they should direct them to Mr Chamberlain himself."

Holmes studied her for a moment, taking in the dark circles under her eyes and the tension in her shoulders. "It must be quite a burden," he said gently, "having to deal with these rumours day in and day out."

The woman's eyes widened in surprise, and for a moment, her guard seemed to drop. "It is," she admitted in a low voice. "Jobs are hard to come by these days, and I can't afford to lose this one. But with all this talk of ghosts and hauntings…" She trailed off, shaking her head.

Watson stepped forward, his kind eyes filled with sympathy. "Rest assured, we're not here to cause any trouble. We simply wish to enjoy the marvels of the museum."

The woman managed a weak smile, clearly appreciating Watson's reassurance. She handed them their tickets. "I hope you enjoy your visit, gentlemen," she said, her voice a little stronger now. "And please, if you do experience anything unusual, let Mr Chamberlain know."

Holmes and Watson thanked her, then turned to enter the museum proper. As Holmes and Watson ventured deeper into the museum, the atmosphere seemed to shift. The grand foyer, with its chequered marble floor and crystal chandelier, gave way to dimly lit corridors lined with velvet ropes and dark wood panelling. The air grew thick with the scent of dust and the faint, persistent odour of chemicals used in the preservation of the wax figures.

The exhibits themselves were a testament to the skill and artistry of their creators. Each scene was meticulously crafted, the wax figures so lifelike that one almost expected them to breathe. In one alcove, King John sat hunched over the Magna Carta, his barons gathered around him in a tableau of historic significance. The figures' faces were painted with such detail that every wrinkle, every line of worry or contemplation, was visible.

As they walked on, Holmes and Watson overheard the hushed conversations of the other visitors. A group of older women huddled together, their glances darting left and right.

"Did you hear about the ghost of an old king?" one of them asked. "They say he moves the figures around at night, rearranging the scenes."

Her friend nodded. "I had heard that. And I'd heard about the strange sounds, too. The moans and whispers. It's like the figures are trying to communicate with us."

Holmes and Watson carried on, passing a display of famous authors. Charles Dickens sat at his desk, pen in hand, his face a mask of concentration. Next to him, a glass case contained a first edition of "A Christmas Carol," open to the page where Marley's ghost first appears to Scrooge.

As they turned a corner, they nearly collided with a man who was hurrying towards the exit, his face pale and his hands shaking.

"Excuse me," Watson said, steadying the man. "Are you all right?"

The man shook his head, his eyes wide with fear. "No," he said, his voice hoarse. "No, I'm not. I saw...I saw something. In the special exhibits room."

Holmes stepped forward. "What did you see, exactly?"

The man swallowed hard, glancing back over his shoulder as if he expected to be followed. "It was in the Egyptian area," he said. "The Sphinx. I swear, I saw it move. And its face changed! Right in front of me. It looked right at me. And then, it smiled. A chilling smile, like it was mocking me."

With that, the man pulled away from Watson's grasp and hurried off, leaving the two investigators standing in the corridor.

"Increasingly intriguing," Holmes mused. "It does make one ponder whether the chap actually witnessed something, or if his imagination, fuelled by the rumours that are widespread in this place, created the alarming visions of its own accord."

They made their way to the special exhibits room, which was currently hosting a display on the wonders of the ancient world. The centrepiece was a scale model of a Sphinx set against a background of scaled-down pyramids, all set on a layer of golden sand. Holmes and Watson approached it, examining it closely.

"I see no signs of movement," Watson said, peering at the model. "And the face looks like those I've seen on such structures before. I can't see anything out of the ordinary here."

Holmes nodded, but his eyes were still scanning the room, taking in every detail. "Perhaps not," he said. "But there's something off about this room. Something is not quite right."

Before Watson could ask him to elaborate, a scream rang out from somewhere deep within the museum. The sound was high and shrill, filled with terror. Around them, visitors began to murmur and shift uneasily.

"Stay here," Holmes told Watson, his voice low and urgent. "Keep an eye on this room. I'm going to investigate."

With that, the Holmes slipped away, disappearing into the shadows of the corridor. Watson watched him go, then turned back to the model of the Sphinx, a frown creasing his brow.

# Chapter 5

Holmes followed the echoes of the scream, his footsteps swift and purposeful against the polished wood floor. The sound led him to an exhibit area where the waxworks of kings and queens stood in regal poses, their faces frozen in expressions of power and authority. Among them, the imposing figure of Henry the Eighth loomed, his broad frame and stern countenance dominating the scene.

At the foot of the display, a pale-faced woman sat on a chair, her hands trembling as her friend wafted a bottle of smelling salts under her nose. Holmes recognised them as the same women who had been ahead of them in the queue earlier. He approached them.

"Pardon me, ladies," he said, "but I heard some screams of distress. Did those screams come from you? If so, might I offer my assistance?"

The seated woman looked up at him, her eyes wide and frightened. "Oh, thank you, sir," she said, her voice quavering. "I'll be all right in a moment. It's just, oh, it was so terrifying."

Holmes knelt beside her. "What happened, exactly?"

The woman took a deep, shuddering breath. "It was the waxwork," she said, pointing a shaking finger at the figure of Henry the Eighth. "I was walking past it, and suddenly I felt this cold draft on the back of my neck. And then...then I heard a voice. It said 'beheaded,' clear as day. It was coming from the figure, I swear!"

Her friend nodded vigorously, her own face pale. "It's true!" she exclaimed. "I heard it too. It must be the ghost of the king who haunts this place. He's threatening to behead any woman who passes by!"

Holmes listened to their story, his expression thoughtful. He knew the power of suggestion could be strong, especially in a place like this where the atmosphere was carefully crafted to unsettle and unnerve. But he kept his thoughts to himself, not wanting to dismiss the women's fears outright.

"That must have been a truly frightening experience," he said, his tone sympathetic.

Just then, a member of the museum staff rushed over, his face etched with worry. "Is everything all right here?" he asked, looking from the women to Holmes.

The seated woman shook her head. "No, it's not," she said, her voice rising. "We were just verbally attacked by the ghost of Henry the Eighth. He threatened to behead us!"

The staff member's eyes widened. "I'm so very sorry," he said. "Is there anything I can do?"

The woman's friend declared, "We want to leave this instant! And you can be sure we'll be telling all our friends about this. This museum is not a safe place to visit, not at all! And we demand a refund."

The employee nodded, helping the seated woman to her feet. As he led the frightened women away, Holmes could hear their voices echoing down the corridor, the dramatic retelling of their experience growing more embellished with each step.

Holmes approached the waxwork of Henry the Eighth, his keen eyes scanning every detail of the figure. The king stood tall and imposing on the raised platform, his broad frame draped in rich velvet and ermine, his face set in a stern expression. Holmes leaned in closer, examining the figure's hands, the folds of its clothing, the texture of its skin. He was looking for anything that might explain the strange occurrence the women had reported.

But try as he might, he could find nothing amiss. The waxwork was expertly crafted. The skin looked almost lifelike; the clothing was historically accurate, and the pose was regal and commanding. There were no obvious signs of tampering, no hidden wires or mechanisms that might account for the ghostly voice. None that he could see, at least.

Frowning, Holmes stepped back and surveyed the other figures in the room. There were other kings and queens here, each standing in line on the same platform. He moved from one to the next, examining each in turn, looking for any anomaly or inconsistency that might provide a clue.

But again, he found nothing. The figures were all of the same high quality as the Henry the Eighth waxwork, their features and clothing rendered with meticulous attention to detail. There were no hidden speakers, no signs of anything unusual.

Holmes stepped back, his brow furrowed in thought. He turned slowly, taking in the entirety of the room. It was a large, high-ceilinged space, with ornate mouldings, heavy velvet drapes, and highly patterned wallpaper. The lighting was dim and atmospheric, designed to showcase the waxworks to their best advantage. And yet, something about the room was bothering him, nagging at the back of his mind.

He couldn't quite put his finger on it, but there was something…off. Something that didn't quite fit. He was about to examine the room more closely, but he heard Watson calling out his name.

"Holmes! Come here! Quickly!"

Holmes rushed into the special exhibit room. He found Watson standing in front of the Sphinx model, his face pale and his eyes wide with shock.

"Watson, what's the matter?" Holmes asked.

Watson raised a trembling finger and pointed at the figure. "I saw it move, Holmes. It shifted slightly to the right, and then…then I saw its face change. From the weathered one that you see now, to a human one. It was a ghostly human face, staring right at me. And, just like that man said earlier, the new face smiled at me; such a chilling smile. The face vanished a moment later."

Holmes frowned, stepping closer to examine the model. "A human face?"

"Yes, I'm certain of it. It was there, as clear as day, and then it was gone." Watson's voice was shaky, but there was a note of anger in it, too.

"And you're sure the Sphinx itself moved?" Holmes asked, looking for disturbances in the sand surrounding the model and finding none.

"Quite sure. It was a subtle movement, but I saw it. I'm certain of that."

Holmes turned to face his friend. "And what do you make of this matter? Has this incident convinced you the museum is haunted?" He waited to hear what the good doctor would say.

All fear left Watson's face. He said, "I don't believe it's haunted whatsoever. This is some kind of trick, an illusion. Something you'd see on the stage. It's all smoke and mirrors, in my opinion."

"I'm glad to hear that," Holmes said. "And whoever is behind this incident is very skilled. They've managed to unsettle even a man of your steadfast nature. If only for a short while."

Watson bristled. "Well, I don't appreciate being the subject of their tricks, skilled or not. It's not right, playing with people's fears like this."

"I agree. And it's our job to expose the truth behind these supposed hauntings. To shed light on the shadows, as it were. Let's examine this room thoroughly, looking for any sign of trickery at work. And we'll talk to the staff, see if anyone else has witnessed these strange occurrences. Also, we need to locate the sculptor with a grudge against Mr Chamberlain, and talk to him."

Watson said, "And what about Mr Chamberlain? Should we inform him of what I saw?"

Holmes paused, considering. "Not yet. I'd like to have a clearer picture of what's going on before we talk to him. For now, we keep this between ourselves."

Watson nodded, trusting his friend's judgement. Together, they began their search, scouring the room for any clue that might shed light on the mysterious events that had just occurred.

# Chapter 6

Holmes and Watson meticulously examined the exhibit room. But despite their thorough search, they found nothing out of the ordinary.

As they moved through the room, Holmes couldn't shake the feeling that he was missing something. It was like a puzzle piece that refused to fit, a clue that danced just beyond his grasp. He frowned as he tried to pin down the elusive thought.

Watson, meanwhile, was growing increasingly uneasy. He kept glancing over his shoulder, his glance darting to the shadowy corners of the room. "Holmes," he said, his voice low and tense, "I feel that we're being watched."

Holmes looked at his friend. He hadn't felt the same sense of unease, but he trusted Watson's instincts. "You think someone is observing us?" he asked.

Watson nodded, his face pale in the dim light. "I can't explain it, but I just have this feeling."

Holmes considered this for a moment. While he didn't share Watson's sense of being watched, he respected his friend's intuition. "Very well," he said. "Let's move on to another exhibit. Perhaps a change of scenery will ease your mind."

They made their way out of the exhibit room and into the next part of the museum, which was a reconstruction of a Victorian street. But this was no ordinary street. It was a dark, grimy alleyway, the kind where criminals and ne'er-do-wells plied their trade. The lighting was dim and flickering, casting eerie shadows on the walls. The air was thick with the smell of fabricated smoke and decay.

Watson looked around, his eyes wide with surprise. He said, "I'm not sure this particular change of scenery has eased my mind at all. I must say, I'm astonished that this is an exhibit. It's all a bit too close to home, isn't it? All the crime and squalor that we see every day in London."

Holmes nodded, his eyes scanning the street with a detective's precision. "Indeed, it is a grim reminder of the underbelly of our city," he said. "But perhaps that is the point. People have a morbid curiosity about the criminal underworld. This exhibit allows them to safely indulge that curiosity, to peer into the shadows without actually stepping into them."

Watson considered this, then nodded slowly. "I suppose you're right. Still, it's an unsettling sight. And this eerie atmosphere... it would be the perfect place for hauntings and spooky noises, wouldn't you say?"

Holmes agreed. "It would. If I were a ghost, or rather, someone pretending to be a ghost, this is precisely the kind of place I would choose to haunt."

They began to walk down the reconstructed street, their footsteps echoing on the cobblestones. On either side, the façades of dilapidated buildings loomed over them, their windows dark and empty. Here and there, shadowy figures could be seen lurking in doorways or crouching in nooks and crannies.

As they moved deeper into the exhibit, Holmes and Watson saw scenes of criminal activity playing out before them. A pickpocket was lifting a wallet from an unsuspecting victim. A con artist was luring a mark into a game of three-card monte. A burglar was jimmying a lock, preparing to break into a shop.

The waxwork figures were incredibly lifelike, their faces etched with malice and greed. Watson shuddered as they passed a particularly menacing figure, a brute of a man with a scar across his cheek and a knife in his hand.

"It's all very impressive," Watson said, "but I must say, it's making me rather uncomfortable. It's like we've stepped into the pages of a penny dreadful."

Holmes, however, seemed fascinated by the exhibit. He was studying each scene with intense concentration, his attention darting from one detail to the next. "Look at the craftsmanship," he murmured. "The attention to detail. These figures are remarkably realistic."

As they turned a corner, they found themselves in a small, dimly lit square. In the centre was a gallows, its noose swaying gently in a breeze. A waxwork figure stood on the platform, a hood over its head, its hands bound behind its back.

Watson swallowed hard. "Good Lord," he whispered. "This is ghastly."

Holmes, however, seemed unperturbed. He approached the gallows, examining the figure with a critical eye. "Fascinating. The sculptor has captured the moment of imminent death with incredible precision. The slump of the shoulders, the limpness of the limbs... it's as if we're looking at a real man."

Watson shook his head, turning away from the grim sight. "I've seen enough," he said. "Let's move on, shall we?"

Holmes and Watson moved away from the grim spectacle of the gallows and made their way back to the dimly lit street.

Despite the unsettling atmosphere, Holmes smiled at the waxwork figures they passed.

"You know, Watson," he said, his voice tinged with amusement, "I'm quite certain I recognise some of the faces portrayed in these criminal waxworks. I think we've helped track down a few of them in our time. I'm sure that man in the long coat over there was responsible for the theft of a racehorse. I wonder if these figures are based on real-life people."

Watson, however, was too nervous to respond. "Holmes," he whispered. "I don't like this at all. It feels like someone is going to jump out at any second."

Holmes opened his mouth to reassure his friend, but before he could speak, a figure suddenly leapt out at them from the shadows. It was the waxwork of Jack the Ripper, his face twisted into a menacing snarl, his knife glinting in the dim light.

Watson let out a scream, stumbling backwards in terror. For a moment, it looked as if he might turn and run, but Holmes quickly placed a steadying hand on his shoulder.

"Easy, old chap," he said, his voice calm and reassuring. "It's all part of the museum's set-up. Look here." He pointed to a section of the street where some of the cobblestones were slightly higher than the others. "When we stepped on these stones, it activated the waxwork of Jack, causing him to move."

Watson let out a nervous laugh, his face flushed with embarrassment. "Of course," he said, shaking his head. "I should have realised."

They watched as the figure of Jack the Ripper retreated back into the shadows, ready to leap out at the next unsuspecting visitor.

Watson shuddered. "Do you think the police will ever catch him, Holmes? Jack the Ripper, I mean."

Holmes considered the question for a moment. "They might," he said, "if they enlisted the help of professional detectives. But I fear Jack is a cunning and elusive quarry. It will take more than the usual methods to bring him to justice. People don't even know what he looks like. But that figure we've just seen could be a reasonable representation."

They continued down the street, the eerie silence broken only by the sound of their footsteps. As they neared the end of the exhibit, Holmes turned to Watson, a curious expression on his face.

"Do you still feel like we're being watched?" Holmes asked.

Watson paused, considering the question. "No," he said, after a moment. "The feeling seems to have passed."

But Holmes shook his head. "On the contrary, Watson," he said, his voice low and serious. "We are being watched. And I know exactly where our observer is."

# Chapter 7

Holmes and Watson emerged from the reconstructed street.

Holmes walked purposely towards a woman standing nearby who was wearing a simple black dress, a white apron, and a white cap atop her soft brown hair, which was tied back in a neat bun. In her hand, she held a cleaning cloth, but she was standing as still as a statue, her eyes wide with wonder as she stared at Holmes.

Holmes smiled at her. "Hello," he said, his voice warm and friendly.

The woman blinked, as if coming out of a trance. "I can't believe it," she whispered, her voice filled with awe. "You're Sherlock Holmes; the great Sherlock Holmes. Right here. Right in front of me. Am I dreaming?"

Holmes smiled and assured she wasn't.

The woman cast a shy smile at Watson, who had joined them and said, "Dr Watson, I've read all your stories. You have such a wonderful way with words. It's such an honour to meet you both."

Watson returned her smile, bowing his head slightly. "The pleasure is ours, Miss..."

"Mrs Eliza Morton," she said, bobbing a curtsey. "I work here at the museum as a cleaner. I suspect you've already worked that out, Mr Holmes, what with your impressive detective skills."

Holmes nodded. "Your attire does give you away, Mrs Morton." He took a moment to study her and placed Eliza Morton in her early forties, with a slim frame and kind, gentle eyes. Her hands were rough from years of work. There was a sadness about her, a sense of loss that seemed to cling to her like a shroud.

Mrs Morton looked from one man to the other, muttering, "I can't believe it, I just can't. The great Sherlock Holmes and Dr Watson. The world's most famous detectives."

Holmes waved away her praise, though he did feel some modicum of pleasure at her words.

She continued talking, "I'm sorry for staring at you so much. It's just that when I saw you both in that street behind you, I thought for a moment that you were waxworks. I was thinking to myself that the sight of you would draw the crowds in for certain, even with all these rumours about hauntings and the suchlike."

Holmes nodded. "We have heard about the rumours. But can you tell us any more about them, Mrs Morton?"

Eliza hesitated, glancing around as if to make sure no one was listening. "Well," she said, lowering her voice, "there have been some strange things happening here at the museum. Visitors have been complaining about feeling cold spots, hearing strange noises, even seeing things move on their own."

Holmes said, "We have heard of similar things. Is there anything else?"

Eliza swallowed nervously. "I shouldn't really be telling you anything. I might lose my job if Mr Chamberlain finds out I've been saying things about his museum. And he's been so kind to me, giving me this job. I lost my husband, Charlie, three years ago to influenza, and working here takes my mind off my grief and my loneliness. I'd be lost without it." Tears sprang to her eyes.

Holmes placed a gentle hand on her shoulder. "I am very sorry to hear about the passing of your husband, Mrs Morton. I wouldn't want to jeopardise your job in any way. It may ease your mind to know that we are here in an official capacity. Mr Chamberlain hired us to investigate the strange activities."

Eliza blinked back her tears. "Oh, Mr Holmes, that is a relief, I can tell you. No doubt, you'll have this mystery cleared up in no time, and then everything can go back to normal."

Holmes retrieved his hand, smiling kindly at the woman. "Now then, Mrs Morton, could you tell us what else you know about the supposed hauntings? If that is okay with you, of course."

Eliza smiled. "It is most certainly okay, Mr Holmes. Well, let me tell you what I know. Only yesterday, I heard a visitor telling her friend that she saw a waxwork figure turn its head and look right at her. Another woman said she heard whispering coming from an empty room. And just the other day, one of the staff found a trail of wax droplets leading from one of the exhibits to the back door. It looked as if someone had carried a melting candle through the museum, but someone said it was a ghost that had left its mark there."

Holmes listened intently. "And have you experienced anything unusual yourself, Mrs Morton?"

Eliza shook her head. "No, sir, and I hope I never do. But I've heard plenty from the other staff. They're all on edge, jumping at shadows and whispering about ghosts and curses. It's not good for business, I can tell you that much."

Dr Watson asked, "And do you believe that these events are paranormal in nature? Do you believe in ghosts, Mrs Morton?"

She shook her head. "I don't. I never have. And anyway, if ghosts were real, and the spirits could talk to us from the other side, wouldn't my Charlie have been in touch with me? Given me a word of comfort or two? But no, once people have passed away, they are gone forever and all they leave behind are the memories we carry in our hearts." She blinked back fresh tears that had appeared.

Holmes smiled kindly at the woman. "Well, Mrs Morton, I must thank you for your candour. I do hope our questions haven't upset you too much. The information you have given us is invaluable."

Eliza beamed, her sadness replaced with pride. "Oh, it's my pleasure, Mr Holmes. Truly, it is. I've always been a great admirer of your work. The way you solve those impossible cases, the way you see things that no one else can...it's just incredible."

Holmes smiled, a rare genuine smile that softened his sharp features. "Thank you, Mrs Morton," he said. "If I may take the liberty of asking you more question, please?"

"Of course." Eliza stood a little taller.

Holmes said, "May I ask which parts of the museum you are responsible for cleaning?"

Eliza's eyes widened slightly at the question, but she answered readily enough. "Why, everywhere, Mr Holmes. From the grand entrance hall to the darkest corners of the exhibits. Even that gruesome street behind us." She shuddered slightly. "I don't much like cleaning there, truth be told. It gives me the shivers, it does."

Holmes nodded. "I can imagine it must be quite unsettling, working in such an atmosphere. Tell me, Mrs Morton, would you be willing to assist us in our investigation?"

Eliza's hand flew to her chest, her face paling. For a moment, it seemed as though she might faint. "Me?" she whispered. "Assist the great Sherlock Holmes?"

Holmes smiled reassuringly. "Indeed, Mrs Morton. You see, in your role as a cleaner, you are uniquely positioned to observe things that others might miss. People tend to overlook those they consider invisible, like yourself, and I mean that with no disrespect whatsoever. People may speak more freely and let their guard down, even though you are nearby."

Eliza nodded slowly, understanding dawning in her eyes. "I see what you mean, Mr Holmes. Yes, people do tend to talk as if I'm not there. As if I'm just another piece of furniture."

"Precisely," Holmes said. "Which is why I believe you could be invaluable to our investigation. I would ask that you keep your eyes and ears open. If you notice any suspicious activity, any odd conversations, anything at all out of the ordinary that you think could help us, I would be most grateful if you could report it to me."

Eliza gave him a firm nod, a look of determination settling over her features. "Of course, Mr Holmes. I'll do whatever I can to help. You can count on me."

Holmes reached into his pocket and withdrew a small card. "Here is my address. Please, feel free to call upon me at any time, day or night, if you have something to report."

Eliza took the card reverently, holding it as if it were a precious gem. "Thank you, Mr Holmes. I'll guard this with my life."

Holmes chuckled. "I don't think that will be necessary. But I do appreciate your dedication."

With a final nod and a smile, Holmes and Watson bade farewell to Eliza Morton and continued on their way through the museum.

As they walked away, Watson looked at his friend. "Holmes, why did you ask Mrs Morton for her help? Surely we can handle this investigation on our own."

Holmes smiled enigmatically. "My dear Watson, you heard what Mrs Morton said. In her role, she is practically invisible. People speak around her as if she's not there. That kind of invisibility can be a powerful tool in our line of work. Never underestimate the power of those who are often overlooked, Watson. They see and hear far more than most people realise. And even I can miss things. That's why it's always good to have an extra set of eyes and ears on a case."

Watson said, "Well, I hope Mrs Morton does hear or see something useful. The sooner we can get to the bottom of this mystery, the better."

Holmes agreed. "But for now, let us continue. I think we have seen enough of the museum for now. It's time to find that sculptor who has a grudge against Mr Chamberlain. I'm interested to hear what he's got to say."

# Chapter 8

Holmes and Watson prepared to seek out the disgruntled sculptor. They didn't get very far before the sound of hurried footsteps echoed through the museum's corridors. They turned to see Alfred Chamberlain approaching them with a look of concern upon his face.

"Mr Holmes, Dr Watson!" Chamberlain called out, his voice tinged with relief. "I've been searching for you, gentlemen. I heard you were in the building."

Holmes raised an eyebrow, his keen eyes taking in Chamberlain's nervous demeanour. "Mr Chamberlain, I trust everything is all right?"

Chamberlain swallowed nervously. "I know I promised you a tour, but might we proceed directly to my office? I'd like to discuss what you've discovered thus far."

Watson exchanged a glance with Holmes, who nodded almost imperceptibly. Watson said, "Of course, Mr Chamberlain. Lead the way."

The trio made their way through the winding corridors of the museum. They soon arrived at Chamberlain's office, a spacious room lined with bookshelves and adorned with various curiosities from around the world. A large mahogany desk dominated the centre of the room, its surface cluttered with papers and ledgers.

Chamberlain gestured for Holmes and Watson to take a seat in the plush armchairs facing his desk. He sank into his own chair, his shoulders sagging as if under a great weight.

"Mr Chamberlain," Holmes began, his voice calm and measured, "Dr Watson and I paid a visit to your ex-business partner, Marcus Bramwell, earlier today."

"And what did he say?"

Holmes said, "Mr Bramwell denies having anything to do with the strange activities occurring in your museum. However, I must confess, I am not entirely convinced of his innocence in this matter."

Chamberlain nodded. "I agree, Mr Holmes. These incidents, they are escalating at an alarming rate. I've had numerous complaints today alone. I fear that if this continues, someone might get physically hurt, and then I'd have no choice but to close the museum immediately. Something that would please Marcus."

Watson said, "Mr Chamberlain, you have our assurance that we will do everything in our power to get to solve this mystery."

Chamberlain managed a weak smile. "Thank you, Dr Watson. I appreciate that more than you know. I need all the help I can get to put a stop to these disturbances, and as quickly as possible."

Holmes studied their client intently. "Mr Chamberlain, I sense there is something weighing on your mind. Something you have not yet shared with us."

Chamberlain shifted uncomfortably in his seat, his eyes avoiding Holmes's penetrating gaze. "I...I don't know what you mean, Mr Holmes."

Holmes said, "Mr Chamberlain, if we are to assist you to the best of our abilities, it is imperative that you are completely honest with us. Even the smallest detail could prove crucial in unravelling this mystery."

Chamberlain's shoulders slumped, and he let out a heavy sigh. He seemed to be wrestling with some internal dilemma.

After a few moments, he reached for a telegram on his desk. He held it up and said, "Mr Holmes, Dr Watson, this arrived less than an hour ago. It's from a woman named Madam Rosalind."

At the mention of the name, Holmes let out a snort of disgust. "I didn't think it would be long until she got in touch," he said, his voice dripping with disdain.

Chamberlain looked at Holmes, curiosity piqued. "I'm aware she's a famous medium, but that's all I know. What can you tell me about her, Mr Holmes?"

Holmes replied, "Madam Rosalind, in my opinion, is nothing but a charlatan, albeit a very skilled one. She has fooled many people into believing she possesses genuine talents, preying upon their grief and vulnerability with her cleverly crafted illusions."

Watson added his thoughts, "I've heard stories of her supposed abilities, but I've always been sceptical. It seems to me that she merely tells people what they wish to hear, offering false comfort for her own gain."

"What does the telegram say, Mr Chamberlain?" Holmes asked.

Chamberlain glanced down at the telegram. "Madam Rosalind claims to have heard about the hauntings and has offered her services to rid the museum of the spirits. She wants to hold a séance."

Holmes raised an eyebrow. "And does she intend to charge for that?"

"No, she doesn't mention any fee," Chamberlain replied, scanning the telegram again. "However, she does request that the press be at the séance. And that I'm to organise that."

A look of understanding dawned on Holmes's face. "Ah, so she's after fame, then. Maybe her present fame isn't enough, and she craves more. Now, this new information makes her a suspect in my eyes."

Watson asked, "You think she might be behind these disturbances, Holmes?"

"It's a possibility we cannot ignore, Watson," Holmes said. "Madam Rosalind has much to gain from associating herself with a high-profile case like this. If she is after fame, as I suspect she might be, Madam Rosalind could have orchestrated this whole affair from the very beginning. She could have asked some of her loyal clients to visit your museum, Mr Chamberlain, and pretend to have seen and felt something strange."

"Ah, I see," Chamberlain said. "But is she capable of such deceit?"

Holmes raised one eyebrow. "Her profession is built on deceit."

Dr Watson cleared his throat, and said, "If I may, Holmes, don't forget what I experienced earlier. I am certainly not working for Madam Rosalind."

Chamberlain asked, "What happened earlier?"

Watson explained about seeing the Sphinx move, and then how the face changed and smiled at him.

"That must have shaken you up, Dr Watson," Chamberlain said. "I'm sorry you had to experience that."

Holmes gave Mr Chamberlain a direct look. "If Madam Rosalind has employed people to discredit your museum, she could also have hired someone working on the inside to help her, too. Someone employed by you."

"Absolutely not!" Chamberlain declared. "I told you earlier that my staff are trustworthy and loyal, and I stand by that."

Holmes thought it wise not to push that point further. Instead, he looked at the telegram and said, "Perhaps you should ask Madam Rosalind to proceed with the séance."

"But why?" Chamberlain asked. "After what you've told me, I'm not sure I want her here."

Holmes nodded. "I agree with you. But by asking her here, the public will see you are doing all you can to put an end to these hauntings. And, more importantly, if she does have people helping to stage these strange occurrences, she may bring them along to the séance and we could catch them in the act."

"Oh, yes, I see what you mean," Chamberlain said with a smile. "I assume you and Dr Watson would like to be at the séance, too?"

Holmes grimaced. "As much as it pains me to say this, yes, I would like to be at the séance held by Madam Rosalind. Could you organise that, Mr Chamberlain?"

"I will reply to her telegram immediately." Chamberlain visibly relaxed. "Is there anything else you can tell me about your investigation so far? Apart from Marcus Bramwell, and now Madam Rosalind, do you have any other suspects?"

"Not yet," Holmes said. He stood up. "But we would like to continue having a look around. I must say, I am extremely impressed with the quality of the waxworks. I'd love to know how they are created. Would it be possible to speak to the sculptors who are behind such works of art?"

"Of course," Chamberlain replied. "My main sculptor is a wonderful chap called Thomas Hargreaves. You'll find him in the workshop area. Let him know I sent you. I'm sure he'll be delighted to tell you more about his work."

He gave Holmes and Watson directions to the workshop and promised to be in touch soon with details of the upcoming séance.

Holmes and Watson walked away from his office.

As soon as they were out of earshot, Watson said, "I wonder if this Thomas Hargreaves is the same sculptor Bramwell told us about, the one who resents Mr Chamberlain. He doesn't sound like it going by Mr Chamberlain's kind words about him."

Holmes smiled at his friend, and said, "We'll soon find out."

# Chapter 9

Holmes and Watson navigated their way through the museum, following the directions provided by Mr Chamberlain. They soon found themselves standing before a sturdy wooden door marked 'Private'. Holmes rapped his knuckles against the door, the sound echoing in the quiet hallway.

Moments later, the door swung open, revealing a man with a friendly face. His eyes crinkled at the corners as he smiled at the two gentlemen. "Good afternoon, sirs. How may I assist you?"

"Good afternoon. I am Sherlock Holmes, and this is my associate, Dr John Watson. We are at the museum on a private matter, and asked Mr Chamberlain if we could learn more about the waxworks and how they are created. He said we should stop by this workshop. We are looking for Thomas Hargreaves."

The man's smile widened. "I'm Thomas Hargreaves. I've worked for Mr Chamberlain since he opened this museum. Before that, I worked for various other museums. Please, come in." He stepped aside, gesturing for them to enter.

As they entered the workshop, Watson let out a gasp. The room was filled with an array of wax figures in various stages of completion. Some were mere skeletons of wire and wood, while others were so lifelike, they seemed poised to draw breath.

"I must say, Mr Hargreaves," Holmes began, his keen eyes scanning the room, "the quality of the waxworks in the museum is truly remarkable. The level of detail and craftsmanship is extraordinary. You are extremely talented."

Thomas beamed with pride. "Thank you, Mr Holmes. I pour my heart and soul into each and every one of these figures. It's not just a job for me; it's a passion."

Holmes nodded. "I can certainly see that. Tell me, how do you go about creating these marvels?"

Thomas clasped his hands together. "Ah, well, the process varies depending on whether the subject is a living person or a historical figure. For living subjects, we begin by taking precise measurements and creating a plaster cast of their face and body."

He led them over to a workbench where a partially completed figure lay. "Once we have the cast, we use it to create a wax positive. This is where the real artistry begins. We sculpt the wax, adding in every detail, from the lines on their face to the texture of their skin."

Holmes leaned in closer, examining the figure. "Fascinating. And what about historical figures?"

"For those, we rely on paintings, photographs, and written descriptions to capture their likeness. It's a bit more challenging, as we have to interpret the information and bring it to life in three dimensions."

Watson pointed to a figure in the corner, dressed in regal attire. "Is that Queen Victoria?"

Thomas nodded. "It is, Dr Watson. Whilst Her Majesty hasn't yet paid a visit to our museum, we are ever hopeful that she will one day. I spent months researching her features and mannerisms to ensure I did her justice."

Holmes circled the figure, his brow furrowed in concentration. "The attention to detail is astounding. The folds of her dress, the expression on her face—it's as if she could step right off the pedestal."

"That's the goal, Mr Holmes," Thomas said, his chest puffing out slightly. "We want our visitors to feel as though they are in the presence of the real person."

Watson turned to Thomas. "How long does it typically take to complete a figure?"

"It varies, but on average, it takes several months. There are many stages involved, from the initial sculpting to the painting and costuming. Each step requires precision and patience."

"And the hair?" Watson asked. "It looks so realistic."

Thomas grinned. "Ah, yes. That's a painstaking process. We use real human hair, which is inserted strand by strand into the wax scalp. It's a time-consuming task, but it makes all the difference in the final product."

As they continued to tour the workshop, Thomas regaled them with stories behind each figure, his enthusiasm infectious. Holmes and Watson listened intently, asking questions and marvelling at the skill and dedication that went into creating these waxen wonders.

"Mr Hargreaves," Holmes said as they prepared to take their leave, "your work is truly exceptional. The museum is fortunate to have an artist of your calibre."

Thomas bowed his head, a slight flush colouring his cheeks. "You're very kind, Mr Holmes. I am grateful for the opportunity to pursue my passion and bring these historical figures to life. I have worked in other museums before this one, but I must say that working for Mr Chamberlain is a real privilege."

Holmes regarded Hargreaves with a thoughtful gaze. "Mr Hargreaves, I hope you don't mind me broaching a rather delicate subject."

Thomas's brow furrowed slightly, but he maintained his friendly demeanour. "Of course not, Mr Holmes. Please, go ahead."

Holmes clasped his hands behind his back, choosing his words carefully. "You might not be aware, but Mr Chamberlain has asked Dr Watson and myself to look into the peculiar occurrences that have been plaguing the museum as of late. The supposed hauntings, if you will."

Thomas replied, "Yes, I have heard the rumours. It's most unsettling for everyone involved."

Watson chimed in, "Have you personally experienced anything unusual, Mr Hargreaves?"

Thomas shook his head. "No, I can't say that I have. You see, I spend most of my time here in the workshop, engrossed in my work. I'm rarely out on the museum floor, except when placing the new figures into place, so I haven't witnessed any of the alleged hauntings first hand."

Holmes said, "And what is your opinion on the matter? Do you believe there could be any truth to these claims of supernatural activity?"

Thomas held up his hands in a gesture of dismissal. "Absolutely not, Mr Holmes. I am a man of reason and logic. I don't put any stock in ghost stories or tales of the paranormal. There must be a rational explanation for whatever is happening."

Holmes nodded. "I agree with you, Mr Hargreaves. Dr Watson and I have always found that the truth lies in the realm of the tangible, not the fantastical. There is another matter I wish to discuss with you. Dr Watson and I recently visited Mr Marcus Bramwell, who is Mr Chamberlain's former business partner. Our visit was in relation to the supposed hauntings."

Thomas's eyebrows shot up in surprise. "Mr Bramwell? I have heard Mr Chamberlain mention him a few times. I'm assuming you considered him a suspect if you visited him. May I ask, what did he have to say?"

Holmes studied Thomas's reaction closely as he continued. "Mr Bramwell made a rather curious claim. He said that a sculptor who worked at this museum was overheard in a public house speaking ill of Mr Chamberlain. I was wondering if you might have any knowledge of this incident."

Thomas's face fell, and he shook his head vehemently. "No, Mr Holmes, I can assure you that I know nothing of the sort. It pains me to think anyone would speak badly of Mr Chamberlain. He has been nothing but kind and supportive to me and my work."

Watson said gently, "We don't mean to imply that you were involved, Mr Hargreaves. We're simply trying to gather all the information we can."

Thomas met Watson's gaze. "I appreciate that, Dr Watson. And I want you both to know that I would never engage in such behaviour. I have the utmost respect for Mr Chamberlain, and I would never dream of disparaging him, especially not in a public setting. That's outrageous!"

Holmes said, "We believe you, Mr Hargreaves. Your dedication to your work and your loyalty to Mr Chamberlain are evident."

Thomas continued, "I can also assure you that I never frequent public houses, as I don't partake in drinking. My evenings are spent here, working on my craft or at home with my family."

Holmes nodded, his expression thoughtful. "Mr Hargreaves, your insight has been invaluable. Before we take our leave, I was wondering if you might have any ideas about who could be behind the strange activities at the museum."

Thomas's brow furrowed, and he seemed to hesitate for a moment. "Well, Mr Holmes, I don't like to speak ill of others, but there is someone who has been quite vocal about his dissatisfaction with the museum as of late."

Watson asked, "Who might that be, Mr Hargreaves?"

"To explain who that might be, I need to take you into another part of the museum," Thomas answered. "It isn't a pleasant area, and it's somewhat ghoulish. Would you like to go there?"

Holmes smiled. "We would, Mr Hargreaves. Please, lead the way."

# Chapter 10

Thomas Hargreaves led Holmes and Watson through the workshop, navigating between the workbenches and shelves laden with tools and supplies. At the back of the room, they reached a large, heavy wooden door.

"Gentlemen," Thomas said, "beyond this door lies a room that some of the employees have taken to calling 'The Crypt'. I must confess, I find the name rather distasteful, but I suppose it does capture the essence of the place."

He reached for the iron handle and pulled the door open with a creak. A gust of cold air rushed up from the depths below, causing the gas lamps on the walls to flicker. Watson shivered involuntarily, pulling his coat tighter around himself.

"I say, it's rather chilly down there, isn't it?" Watson remarked.

Holmes, however, seemed unperturbed by the drop in temperature. His keen eyes were fixed on the stone steps that descended into the darkness. "Shall we?" he said, gesturing for Thomas to lead the way.

Thomas nodded and began the descent, the sound of his footsteps echoing off the damp walls. Holmes and Watson followed close behind, the cold air nipping at their faces as they ventured deeper into the bowels of the museum.

At the bottom of the stairs, Thomas lit several more lamps, illuminating the vast cellar. Watson's eyes widened as he took in the sight before him. The room was filled with an assortment of waxwork figures in various states of disrepair. Some stood intact, their blank eyes staring into the void, while others were mere torsos or disembodied limbs scattered across the stone floor.

"Good Lord," Watson breathed. "It's like a macabre version of a sculptor's studio."

Thomas nodded, a wry smile playing on his lips. "This is where we store the figures that are no longer needed for display. Some will be repurposed, their parts used to create new characters. Others, I'm afraid, are destined for the melting pot, their wax to be reused in future creations."

Holmes moved through the room, his keen eyes taking in every detail. He paused beside a table where several wax heads were lined up, their expressions frozen in various states of emotion.

"Fascinating," Holmes murmured, lifting one of the heads to examine it more closely.

Thomas joined Holmes at the table, ready to answer any questions he might have.

Watson, meanwhile, had wandered to the far end of the cellar, where a group of figures stood in a semicircle, their poses suggesting they had once been part of a larger tableau. As he approached, a floorboard creaked beneath his feet, the sound echoing through the cavernous space. He froze, his heart pounding in his chest. "This place is rather unsettling," he called out to Holmes and Thomas. "It's as if the figures are watching us, even in their current state."

Holmes chuckled softly. "Come now, Watson. You know as well as I do that these are merely inanimate objects, devoid of any real consciousness."

Despite Holmes's reassurance, an expression of unease settled on Watson's face.

Thomas, sensing Watson's discomfort, offered a sympathetic smile. "I understand your apprehension, Dr Watson. It takes some getting used to, being surrounded by these figures. But I assure you, there is nothing to fear down here."

Holmes, having completed his inspection of the heads, turned to face Thomas. "Mr Hargreaves, you mentioned earlier that there was someone who had been vocal about their dissatisfaction with the museum. I believe you were about to tell us who that might be."

Thomas Hargreaves led Holmes and Watson to a corner of the cellar where a solitary figure stood, its features obscured by shadows. As they approached, Thomas reached out and turned the figure to face them, revealing the waxen likeness of a man in a tailcoat and top hat, his hands poised as if in the midst of a magic trick.

"Gentlemen, allow me to introduce you to Quentin Silverstone," Thomas said, a note of weariness in his voice.

Holmes studied the figure. "Ah, yes. The stage magician, Quentin Silverstone. I've seen his name emblazoned on playbills around the city, though I must confess I've never attended one of his performances myself. I assume there must be a reason why his likeness has now been placed down here."

Thomas explained, "Mr Silverstone was quite popular when the museum first opened. His figure was prominently displayed, and visitors were drawn to his likeness.

However, something happened at the theatre where he performed recently that caused his popularity to wane."

Watson raised an eyebrow. "What sort of incident, Mr Hargreaves?"

Thomas shrugged. "I'm not entirely sure of the details, Dr Watson. Rumours circulated about a trick gone wrong, or perhaps a scandal involving Mr Silverstone. Whatever the case, the theatre-goers began to avoid his shows, and Mr Chamberlain decided it was time to remove his figure from the main exhibition."

Holmes circled the waxwork. "And how did Mr Silverstone react to this decision?"

Thomas replied, "He was furious, Mr Holmes. He came to the museum and caused quite a scene in front of the visitors. He demanded to speak with Mr Chamberlain, and when he arrived, Quentin threatened him with all sorts of dire consequences if his figure wasn't reinstated immediately."

Watson's eyes widened. "He threatened Mr Chamberlain? In public?"

Thomas nodded. "He did. It was a most unpleasant spectacle. Mr Chamberlain tried to reason with him, explaining that the museum had to adapt to the changing tastes of the public, but Mr Silverstone wouldn't hear of it."

Holmes paused in his examination of the figure. "And has Mr Silverstone returned to the museum since then?"

"Oh, yes," Thomas said. "He comes back every day, demanding to see if his figure has been returned to its former place of honour. Each time, he grows more agitated when he discovers it hasn't."

Watson shook his head. "It sounds like the man has quite the temper. Holmes, do you think he could be responsible for the strange occurrences in the museum?"

Holmes tapped his chin thoughtfully. "It's a possibility, Watson. A man with a wounded ego and a flair for the dramatic could certainly be capable of staging such events. But we mustn't jump to conclusions just yet. Mr Hargreaves, what do you intend to do with Quentin's figure now that it has been removed from display?"

Thomas glanced at the waxwork, a hint of uncertainty in his eyes. "To be honest, Mr Holmes, I'm not entirely sure. It's possible that the figure will be repurposed, its parts used to create a new character. Or, if Mr Chamberlain decides it's no longer needed, it may be melted down, and the wax reused for future projects. Going by how upset Mr Chamberlain was after Quentin yelled at him, this waxwork is most likely to be melted."

Holmes said, "I see. And does Mr Silverstone know of these potential fates for his likeness?"

"No, sir," Thomas replied. "Given his current state of agitation, we thought it best to keep such details private. But considering what has been going on in the museum, these so-called hauntings, I wonder if Mr Silverstone has already found out and is taking revenge."

Watson shifted uneasily. "Holmes, if Mr Silverstone were to discover his figure might be destroyed, it could push him over the edge. A man with his temperament, faced with the prospect of his own destruction, even in effigy..."

"It's a delicate situation and one we must handle with the utmost care," Holmes said. "Mr Hargreaves, I trust you will keep this information about Quentin's waxwork confidential for the time being?"

Thomas nodded solemnly. "Of course, Mr Holmes."

Holmes asked, "Do you have any other people in mind who could be behind the activities, apart from Quentin Silverstone?"

Thomas shook his head. "None that I know of."

Holmes gave Thomas a card and said, "If you do think of anyone, please let us know. And if you discover any information that may be relevant to our enquiries, we would appreciate it if you could call on us."

Thomas said he would.

Holmes thanked him for his time, and with Watson at his side, they ascended the steps and entered the relative cheeriness of the workshop again.

A few minutes later, Holmes and Watson left the museum and walked away from it.

Watson shivered and said, "No wonder they call that cellar, 'The Crypt.' What a dreadful place. Where shall we go now, Holmes? Seek out Quentin Silverstone, I presume?"

Holmes came to a sudden stop, his attention on someone across the road. He said, "We will visit Mr Silverstone in due course, but first, I would like to speak to that person across the street there."

Watson looked at where Holmes had his attention. "By Jove! What is he doing here?"

# Chapter II

Holmes and Watson studied the man across the street. It was Marcus Bramwell. He was intently focused on a notebook, his hand moving deftly across the page. Holmes' keen eyes narrowed as he observed the scene.

"Watson," he said, "it appears that Mr Bramwell is sketching something. His attention appears to be on Mr Chamberlain's Waxwork Museum, but I could be mistaken. I suggest we approach him discreetly from behind to ascertain the subject of his drawing."

Watson nodded, and the two men crossed the road, careful to remain out of Bramwell's line of sight. As they drew nearer, they could see the unmistakable outline of the Waxwork Museum taking shape on the page. However, there was one striking difference: the name 'Alfred Chamberlain' had been replaced by 'Marcus Bramwell'.

Before either of them could comment, Bramwell spoke without turning around. "Good day, Mr Holmes, Dr Watson. I trust you're both well?"

Holmes raised an eyebrow. "You recognised us without even turning around, Mr Bramwell. Impressive."

Bramwell tapped the ground with his foot, indicating the shadows cast by the detective and his companion. "Your silhouettes are quite distinctive. Now, to what do I owe the pleasure of your company?"

"We were about to ask you the same question," Holmes replied, stepping forward. "What brings you to this area, and why have you replaced Mr Chamberlain's name with your own in your sketch?"

Marcus closed his notebook and turned to face them. "Ah, straight to the point, Mr Holmes. I admire that about you."

Watson interjected, "Are you planning to force Mr Chamberlain to sell you the museum, Mr Bramwell? Are you drawing up plans for the changes you will make once it is yours?"

Bramwell laughed. "Dr Watson, you do have a vivid imagination. No, I have no intention of forcing anyone to do anything. However, I do believe this conversation should be continued in a more private setting. Might I suggest we adjourn to The King's Arms? It's just around the corner, and they serve an excellent pint."

Holmes studied Bramwell for a moment, trying to discern his true intentions. The man's demeanour was calm and collected, giving nothing away. Finally, he nodded. "Very well, Mr Bramwell. We will go with you."

A short while later, they entered The King's Arms, a cosy establishment with a warm, inviting atmosphere. Bramwell led them to a quiet corner table and signalled to the barman for a round of drinks.

Once they were settled, Holmes said, "Now, Mr Bramwell, perhaps you could enlighten us as to your interest in the Waxwork Museum and your reasons for altering Mr Chamberlain's name in your sketch."

Bramwell replied, "I have always been a man with an eye for opportunity. The Waxwork Museum is not reaching its full potential under Alfred's management. I believe that with my expertise and vision, I could elevate it to new heights. With all the rumours of hauntings taking place within the building, I suspect Mr Chamberlain will be forced to close the museum soon. That will give me the perfect opportunity to purchase it. And when that happens, I will use all my business expertise to make sure I get it at a low price. I'll make Mr Chamberlain an offer that he can't refuse, not in the circumstances."

Holmes said, "Would you be responsible for those rumours?"

Bramwell shook his head. "My old friend, Chamberlain, has brought this on himself. As you will find out if you ever solve this case and discover who is benefiting from these disturbances. I assume you are further on in your investigation, Mr Holmes? Or could this be the case that finally stumps the great Sherlock Holmes?"

Watson bristled at Bramwell's mocking words and retorted, "I assure you, Mr Bramwell, that Holmes is more than capable of solving this case. He has tackled far more complex mysteries with great success."

Holmes, however, remained unperturbed. He studied Bramwell with a calm, analytical gaze. "The case is proceeding quite well, Mr Bramwell. However, your professional history with Mr Chamberlain intrigues me, in particular, why you are no longer business partners. Any information you could provide on that matter would be most appreciated."

At that moment, their pints arrived, carried by a young barmaid with rosy cheeks and bright eyes. Bramwell flashed her a charming smile, causing her to blush deeply.

"Thank you, my dear," he said smoothly, his smile lingering as she hurried away.

Bramwell took a long, slow sip of his pint, savouring the flavour. He set the glass down and fixed Holmes with a condescending look. "Very well. I shall enlighten you about my falling out with Chamberlain, if only to aid your clearly floundering investigation."

He leaned forward, his elbows resting on the table. "Alfred and I were once partners, as you know. We created many small businesses that performed well. It soon came to our attention that a waxworks museum could be extremely lucrative, so we began to take steps to make that happen. We had grand plans to create the most spectacular and innovative museum London had ever seen. However, it soon became apparent that Chamberlain lacked the vision and ambition necessary to achieve true greatness. He was content with mediocrity, satisfied with the status quo. I, on the other hand, saw the potential for much more. I wanted to push the boundaries, to create displays that would astound and amaze the public. But Chamberlain, in his narrow-mindedness, refused to see the merit in my ideas."

Holmes and Watson remained silent, waiting for Marcus Bramwell to continue talking.

And talk he did.

Bramwell took another swig of his pint, his eyes narrowing. "We argued constantly, our differing philosophies driving a wedge between us. Finally, I could take it no more. I severed our partnership and struck out on my own, determined to prove that my vision was the true path to success. To my great annoyance, he used the plans that we had drawn up together as the basis for his new waxworks museum, thus bringing some parts of my vision to life without giving me any credit. Which is why I never went ahead with my own waxwork museum and settled on creating a science-based one instead. Chamberlain betrayed me. Something I'll never forgive him for."

Bramwell fell silent and looked into his nearly empty glass. A slow smile spread across his face.

Holmes said to Bramwell, "I sense you have something else you wish to share."

Bramwell looked up, a malicious gleam in his eyes. "I am still furious with that man. And yet, it warms my heart to know that Chamberlain's business is floundering, while mine is thriving. It is only a matter of time before he is forced to sell, and when he does, I shall be there to pick up the pieces and mould them into something truly magnificent."

"I see," Holmes said. "And you believe that these rumours will be the undoing of Mr Chamberlain's museum?"

Bramwell chuckled. "Undoubtedly. The public is fickle, Mr Holmes. They crave sensation and spectacle, but they are easily frightened. It won't be long until they will stay away in droves. And when Chamberlain is desperate, I shall swoop in and acquire the property for a fraction of its true value."

Watson frowned. "That seems a rather underhanded way to go about business, Mr Bramwell."

Bramwell shrugged, unconcerned. "Business is not for the faint of heart, Dr Watson. One must be ruthless if one wishes to succeed. I make no apologies for my methods."

He drained the last of his pint and set the glass down with a thud. "Now, if you'll excuse me, gentlemen, I have other matters to attend to. I trust our conversation has been enlightening, and I wish you the best of luck in your investigation. Though, from what I've seen, you'll need more than luck to solve this case."

With a final, arrogant smile, Bramwell rose from his seat and strode out of the pub, leaving Holmes and Watson to ponder his words.

Before Holmes and Watson could discuss their conversation with Bramwell, an older man with ruddy cheeks approached their table looking apprehensive. He said, "Mr Holmes, is it?"

Holmes nodded. "It is. Can I help you?"

The man glanced toward the door. "Mr Bramwell spotted me on his way out. We know each other. He comes in here sometimes, and we often have a chat, setting the world to rights, that sort of thing. Well, just now, Mr Bramwell said I was to come over here and talk to you. He said I know something that will help you."

# Chapter 12

"Please, have a seat," Holmes said. "And your name is?"

The man sat down and said, "George. George Smithson."

Holmes smiled. "A pleasure to meet you, Mr Smithson. Now, what is it you wish to tell us?"

George began, "Well, it's about a friend of mine, Thomas Hargreaves. He works at Mr Chamberlain's Waxworks Museum."

Holmes' brow furrowed. He described Thomas Hargreaves as they had met him earlier - a genial, welcoming man who took pride in his work. "Is this the same Thomas Hargreaves?"

George nodded. "The very same. He comes here almost every night, right after work. But not tonight. His wife put her foot down, demanded he come home early and spend time with the family for a change."

Watson said, "But Thomas told us he never drinks."

George burst into laughter, the sound ringing through the pub. "Never drinks? That's a good one. Thomas is here more often than not, complaining about his job over a pint or three. The more he drinks, the more he complains."

Holmes said, "And why did Marcus Bramwell ask you to speak with us?"

George shifted uncomfortably in his seat. "Like I said, Thomas is always going on about how terrible it is working at the museum. He says Mr Chamberlain is a right tyrant, never appreciating the work Thomas does. I mentioned it to Bramwell a while back during one of our chats. He seemed mighty pleased to hear that Chamberlain's employees were unhappy. I didn't give him Thomas' name because I didn't want Thomas to get into trouble. But I did tell Mr Bramwell that it was a sculptor at the museum who'd been complaining. Afterwards, I felt so bad talking about Thomas like that. But it's the beer, you see, it always loosens my tongue."

"I understand, George," Holmes said. "Could you tell us exactly what Thomas told you? Mr Bramwell is right that it would help us."

George hesitated, but under Holmes' unwavering gaze, he relented. "He was always going on about how he's the real talent behind the waxworks, but Chamberlain takes all the credit. Says his sculptures are the only reason people come to the museum, but Chamberlain treats him like dirt and it would serve him right if Thomas left."

"Anything else?" Holmes prompted.

Charlie said, "Well, Thomas talked about getting his revenge on Chamberlain. Saying things like 'Chamberlain will get what's coming to him' and 'One day, he'll regret treating me like this'. It's all a bit unsettling, if you ask me."

Holmes and Watson exchanged a meaningful glance. This information shed new light on the case, suggesting that the disturbances at the museum might not be the work of a rival, but of a disgruntled employee after all.

"Has he ever mentioned anything specific?" Watson asked. "Any plans or ideas about how he might seek this revenge?"

George shook his head. "No, nothing specific. Just a lot of dark muttering and ominous statements. I always thought it was just the drink talking, but with all these strange things happening at the museum. Well, it makes you wonder, doesn't it?"

"Thank you, Mr Smithson," Holmes said. "You've been most helpful. We may need to speak with you again. Is there a way we can contact you?"

George waved his arm around the pub. "You'll usually find me here. This is a second home to me, that's what my wife says, anyway. You'll find Thomas here tomorrow night, too. Shall I tell him I've been talking to you?"

"I'd rather you didn't," Holmes replied. "We'll be talking to Mr Hargreaves soon about his threats, but we won't let on it was you who told us."

"I appreciate that," George said. He stood up and walked away, slightly unsteady on his feet.

As Holmes and Watson made their way out of the pub later on, Holmes said, "It seems our Mr Hargreaves has been leading us a merry dance. I wonder what else he has been lying about."

Watson nodded. "Do you think he's behind this haunting business?"

"He could very well be," Holmes surmised. "Let's see if we can catch him at the museum now and have another chat with him. Although, I fear the museum may now be closed at this late hour."

Holmes was correct, and it was with dismay that they stopped outside the museum's door and looked at the 'Closed' sign.

"Never mind," Holmes said briskly. "Hargreaves told us that Quentin Silverstone could be a suspect in this matter.

We shall visit Mr Silverstone now and see what he tells us. However, it could turn out that Mr Hargreaves lied about him, too."

# Chapter 13

Holmes and Watson made their way through the bustling theatre district, the streets lined with grand, ornate buildings and the air filled with the excited chatter of theatregoers. Billboards and posters adorned the walls, announcing the latest shows and the brightest stars of the stage.

After a few minutes of searching, they found the theatre they were looking for. 'Quentin Silverstone: The Final Curtain,' it proclaimed in bold, red letters on a poster outside the building.

"Looks like we're just in time for his last performance," Holmes remarked as they approached the ticket booth. "I wonder if he's taking early retirement, or if there is something else in play here."

"Two tickets for Quentin Silverstone's show, please," Watson said to the cashier. "And if possible, we'd like to speak with Mr Silverstone after the performance."

The woman in the ticket booth handed over the tickets, but before she could speak, a man standing nearby stepped forward and introduced himself. "Reginald Barclay, theatre manager. May I ask why you wish to speak with Mr Silverstone?"

"It's a private matter, Mr Barclay," Holmes replied politely. "We have some questions for him regarding an ongoing investigation."

Barclay nodded, then gestured for them to follow him to a quieter corner of the lobby, away from the bustling crowd of eager theatregoers. "I must warn you, gentlemen," he said in a low voice, "Mr Silverstone is not in the best of moods. I'm not sure he will even speak to you. This is to be his final performance, and it weighs heavily upon him."

"We noticed it was his final show from the poster outside," Watson said. "Could you tell us why?"

Barclay sighed. "His act has been slipping as of late. Too many mistakes on stage, and he's lost his touch with the audience. They no longer gasp in wonder at his illusions; instead, they whisper and laugh when he falters. The younger magicians, with their new tricks and daring stunts, are outshining him, and he knows it all too well."

"Has he said anything about this?" Holmes asked.

"Oh, he never stops complaining," Barclay said, shaking his head in exasperation. "Always going on about how these young upstarts don't know true magic, and how they've stolen his tricks. It's a constant refrain with him these days. And he's been particularly bitter about his waxwork figure being removed from that museum not far away. You'd think the manager of it had personally insulted him, the way he carries on about it. But I suppose when your star is fading, every slight cuts a bit deeper."

"His waxwork figure?" Watson asked in all innocence.

Barclay's expression turned sombre as he recounted the events. "Yes, he used to have a figure in Chamberlain's Waxwork Museum. Was quite proud of it, too. But they took it down in recent weeks. He's been in a foul mood ever since. Quentin has worked for me for years and I feel awful about letting him go. But I had no other choice. The audience complained after his every performance and demanded refunds. And my other acts also complained because they were on the receiving end of Quentin's constant criticism."

"Interesting," Holmes said. "Well, thank you for your time, Mr Barclay."

Barclay gave them a grim smile. "Enjoy the show, gentlemen. Though I fear it may not be the grand finale Mr

Silverstone had hoped for. Out of respect for Quentin, I will be watching it, too."

Holmes and Watson made their way into the theatre. The auditorium was sparsely populated, with only a handful of people scattered among the seats. They found their places just as the lights began to dim.

Mr Barclay took a standing position at the side of the seats, his face set in a frown.

The curtains slowly opened, revealing a stage set with various pieces of equipment. A sense of anticipation hung in the air, tinged with a hint of unease.

As the spotlight illuminated the centre of the stage, Holmes leaned over to Watson. "Let's see just how bad this performance will be," he whispered. "And more importantly, what it might tell us about our Mr Silverstone's state of mind."

Watson nodded, his eyes fixed on the stage as they waited for the magician to make his appearance.

The theatre lights dimmed a little and Quentin Silverstone made his grand entrance. He strode onto the stage with a confident smile, his tailored suit and top hat impeccable and his eyes gleaming with anticipation. Despite the sparse audience, Quentin greeted them warmly, his voice carrying through the auditorium with a practised ease.

"Ladies and gentlemen, I thank you for parting with your hard-earned money to witness the wonders I have in store for you tonight," he said, his tone both gracious and assured. "I promise you an evening of magic and illusion that will leave you breathless."

Holmes and Watson exchanged a glance, both surprised by Quentin's confident demeanour. They had expected a bitter, resentful man, but the magician before them exuded a professional air that belied the rumours of his decline.

As the show began, Quentin launched into a series of mesmerising tricks that held the small audience spellbound, with Holmes being the one exception.

Quentin started with a classic sleight of hand, producing a flurry of playing cards from thin air. The cards danced between his fingers, vanishing and reappearing in a dizzying display of dexterity. The audience gasped and applauded, their eyes wide with wonder.

Next, Quentin called for a volunteer from the audience. A young woman, her face flushed with excitement, made her way to the stage. Quentin presented her with a simple wooden box, inviting her to examine it closely. Satisfied that it was indeed ordinary, she handed it back to him. With a flourish, Quentin closed the lid and tapped it three times with his wand. When he opened the box again, a couple of white doves burst forth, their wings fluttering as they soared over the audience's heads. The young woman clapped her hands in delight, and the audience erupted in applause.

Quentin's performance continued, each illusion more impressive than the last. He conjured bouquets of flowers from empty vases, levitated a table with a mere gesture, and even made his assistant disappear and reappear on the other side of the stage. Throughout the show, Quentin's confidence never wavered. His movements were precise, his patter engaging, and his illusions flawless.

In the audience, the theatre manager watched with a look of growing astonishment. It was clear he had expected Quentin to falter, to make the mistakes that had plagued his recent performances. But tonight, the magician was in top form, his act as polished as it had been in his prime.

As the show reached its climax, Quentin announced his final trick—escaping from the water torture cell. A large, glass tank was wheeled onto the stage, filled to the brim with water. Quentin's assistant helped him into a straitjacket. With a dramatic flourish, Quentin was lowered into the tank, the lid locked above him.

The audience held their breath as they watched Quentin struggle against his bonds, bubbles rising from his mouth as he fought to free himself. Seconds ticked by, turning into minutes. Just when it seemed all hope was lost, the lid of the tank burst open, and Quentin emerged, gasping for air but triumphant. The straitjacket hung loosely from his shoulders, proving his skill as an escape artist.

The small audience leapt to their feet, their applause thunderous despite their few numbers. Quentin took his bows, his face beaming with pride. As he exited the stage, the theatre manager rushed towards the backstage area, grinning with delight.

Watson exclaimed, "Well! That was quite a show. Not at all what I was expecting."

Holmes nodded. "I don't think the manager was expecting that either. Did you see the way he dashed towards the backstage area? No doubt, after that performance, he will be asking Quentin Silverstone to stay."

"But why the sudden change in his performance?" Watson wondered.

Holmes stood. "That's what we are going to find out. Come, Watson, let's make our way to Mr Silverstone's dressing room."

"Do you think he could be responsible for those occurrences at the museum?" Watson asked as he followed

Holmes. "He certainly knows enough tricks to create such effects, I would imagine."

"We should certainly consider him a suspect, but let's hear what he's got to say about the museum first. I'm also intrigued as to why his performance was better than what everyone, including the manager, was expecting."

# Chapter 14

Holmes and Watson went backstage. They were greeted by a bustling scene of activity. Performers of all kinds were preparing for their time in the spotlight. Acrobats stretched and limbered up, their sequined costumes glinting under the dim lights. Jugglers practised their routines, the colourful balls and clubs arcing through the air with precision. Dancers applied their stage makeup, turning their faces into works of art.

Amidst this whirlwind of preparation, Holmes and Watson spotted Quentin's dressing room. The door was slightly ajar, and the sound of animated conversation spilled out into the corridor. They approached cautiously, positioning themselves just out of sight, their ears straining to catch every word.

"Quentin, my dear fellow!" Mr Barclay's voice was effusive with praise. "That was a magnificent performance! I must admit, I had my doubts, but you've proven me wrong in the most spectacular fashion."

Quentin's laughter was warm and genuine. "Thank you, Mr Barclay. I know my recent performances have been lacking, and I apologise for that. But I've had a change of heart, a new perspective on life and my craft."

"Well, it's working wonders! The audience was absolutely enthralled. I haven't seen a response like that in years."

Quentin said, "It's all thanks to a wise woman who helped me see things differently. She made me realise that my bitterness and resentment were holding me back, both on stage and off."

Mr Barclay replied, "A wise woman? Who is she? Do I know her?"

"Ah, that's a story for another time, my friend. Suffice it to say, she helped me remember why I fell in love with magic in the first place. The joy of creating wonder, of making the impossible seem possible, if only for a moment."

"Well, I'm glad she did. And I'm glad you've found your passion again. Which brings me to my next point. Quentin, I know we had discussed this being your final performance, but after tonight, I simply can't let you go.

The theatre needs you, the audience needs you. Would you consider staying on?"

There was a pause, and Holmes could almost picture Quentin's thoughtful expression.

"Mr Barclay, I would be honoured to continue performing here. And I promise, from this moment on, I will give every show my all. No more half-hearted efforts, no more bitter complaints. I will be the magician this theatre deserves."

"Excellent! I couldn't be happier to hear that. And Quentin, I want you to know that I understand the pressures of this business. If you ever need to talk, my door is always open."

"Thank you, I appreciate that. And I want to apologise for my behaviour these past few weeks, perhaps months! I know I've been difficult to work with, and I've likely upset quite a few people. I intend to make amends, to apologise to everyone I've wronged."

"That's a noble sentiment, Quentin. I'm sure they will appreciate it. Now, I must be off. I have a theatre to run, after all! But again, congratulations on a stunning performance. I look forward to many more."

The sound of footsteps approached the door, and Mr Barclay emerged, a broad smile on his face. He nodded to Holmes and Watson as he passed, his eyes alight with satisfaction. He said, "I'm sure Mr Silverstone would love to talk to you. He's in excellent spirits!"

The manager hastened away, still smiling.

Holmes knocked on the open door and entered the room with Watson at his side. The dressing room was a cosy space, filled with the trappings of a magician's trade. A large mirror adorned one wall, surrounded by bright bulbs. Costumes hung on a rack, their sequins and silks catching the light. A table was littered with an assortment of props - playing cards, silk scarves, and mysterious boxes with hidden compartments.

Quentin, now changed into dry clothes following his escape from the water tank, greeted them with a smile. "Ah, Mr Holmes and Dr Watson! I thought I recognised you in the audience. What brings you backstage?"

Holmes returned the smile. "Mr Silverstone, we were hoping you could help us with an investigation we are dealing with."

Quentin's eyes sparkled with interest. "But of course! I would love to be of assistance. Please, take a seat." He gestured to some plush armchairs.

As they settled in, Holmes began, "We are currently dealing with a case that involves so-called hauntings. There have been reports of ghostly figures, objects moving on their own, and disembodied voices."

Quentin nodded. "Hauntings? How fascinating."

Holmes proceeded to give more details. "In one instance, a statue-like figure was reported to have moved its head and spoken. In another, a cold wind was felt, and a threatening message was heard. What I'm curious about, Mr Silverstone, is whether someone with your skills, say an experienced magician, would be capable of achieving such things."

Quentin sat back, a thoughtful expression on his face. "It's certainly possible, Mr Holmes. We magicians are masters of illusion, after all. While I can't give away my secrets, I can tell you that those effects you mentioned could be achieved through clever staging and misdirection."

"Please, do elaborate," Holmes encouraged.

"Well, take the moving figure, for example. With the right mechanisms hidden inside the figure, or around the outside, it could be made to move subtly. A hidden phonograph could provide the voice. As for the cold wind and the message, a well-placed fan and a concealed speaker could create that illusion."

Watson looked impressed. "That's ingenious!"

Quentin smiled modestly. "It's all part of the craft, Dr Watson. We magicians spend years perfecting these techniques to create the illusion of the impossible."

Holmes nodded. "And what about the ghostly figures that have been sighted?"

"Ah, there are several ways to achieve that effect. Pepper's ghost illusion is a classic; using angled glass and carefully placed lighting to create a ghostly apparition. Or, with the right costume and makeup, an actor could pass for a spectral figure in the right setting."

"Fascinating," Holmes said. "This sheds new light on our investigation."

Quentin leaned forward conspiratorially. "Mr Holmes, if you don't mind me asking, where exactly are these hauntings taking place?"

"At the Chamberlain Waxworks Museum," Holmes responded.

Quentin's expression shifted, a flicker of discomfort crossing his features. He leaned back in his chair, a sigh escaping his lips. "Ah, the Chamberlain Waxworks Museum," he said, his voice tinged with regret. "I must confess, gentlemen, I have made quite a spectacle of myself there recently.

"The museum used to have a waxwork figure of me, a representation of my craft and my fame. I was proud of it, perhaps too proud. But some weeks ago, I discovered that it had been removed, replaced by a figure of a new and upcoming magician. I was furious, absolutely livid. I demanded that my figure be reinstated, that my legacy be respected. I'm ashamed to admit it now, but I caused quite a scene. My behaviour was unacceptable, and I deeply regret it. I intend to visit the museum soon, to apologise to everyone I've upset, including Mr Chamberlain himself."

Holmes said, "That's admirable of you. I'm sure Mr Chamberlain and his staff would appreciate your apology. Mr Silverstone, we spoke with your manager, Mr Barclay, before your performance. He warned us that your performance would not be up to your usual standard, hence the reason for it being your last performance. But Mr Barclay was impressed by your act, as were the audience. I couldn't help but overhear his conversation with you just now, and how he has asked you to stay at the theatre. Might I ask what prompted this transformation in yourself that has led to your renewed success?"

Quentin's face softened. "Ah, Mr Holmes, it's all down to an amazing woman. She has shown me the error of my ways, helped me see the world in a new light. She has been my saviour."

Holmes said, "Really? And who might this enigmatic woman be?"

Quentin's gaze drifted towards the open door of his dressing room. "She's here now, as a matter of fact."

# Chapter 15

Holmes and Watson turned to look at the person behind them.

Quentin rose, held out his hands and said, "Madam Rosalind, what a delight to see you again so soon."

Madam Rosalind entered the room, the silver embroidery on her flowing purple dress sparkling brightly. Her long, dark hair framed her striking face and intelligent green eyes. A large crystal pendant hung from her neck, catching the light as she moved with otherworldly grace.

"Quentin, my darling man," Madam Rosalind said as she placed her delicate hands in his, her voice smooth as silk and imbued with a captivating charm. "Your performance was absolutely mesmerising. The audience was spellbound by your illusions and the mastery with which you executed them. I have no doubt that your star will rise higher than ever before, and your name will be spoken with reverence in the halls of magic."

Quentin beamed at her praise, his eyes alight with gratitude and a touch of pride. "Thank you, Madam Rosalind. Your guidance has been invaluable to me. I could not have achieved such a change without your wisdom and support. I am forever in your debt."

Madam Rosalind bestowed a gracious smile upon Quentin and smoothly removed her hands from his. She turned her attention to Holmes, a smile playing on her lips. "Ah, the famous Sherlock Holmes. It has been far too long since our paths last crossed. I have missed you. And Dr Watson, is it my imagination or have you become more handsome since we last met."

Watson cleared his throat and said stiffly, "Good evening, Madam Rosalind."

Holmes said nothing at all; his face was devoid of any emotion.

Madam Rosalind said softly, "My dear Sherlock, as I walked down the hallway mere moments ago, I overheard your conversation about Chamberlain's Waxwork Museum. I believe I may be the one to solve this mystery of yours."

Holmes raised an eyebrow. "Is that so? May I ask how?"

She stepped closer, her robes swishing around her ankles. "I have offered to hold a séance at the museum, to communicate with the restless spirits and guide them to move on. Mr Chamberlain has graciously accepted my offer. I received a telegram from him about an hour ago."

Quentin looked intrigued. "A séance. How fascinating!"

Madam Rosalind nodded. "The spirit world is a mysterious and complex realm. It takes a skilled medium to navigate its depths and bring peace to troubled souls."

Holmes remained sceptical as ever. "And you believe you possess such skills, Madam Rosalind?"

She laughed, a melodic sound that filled the room, her eyes sparkling with amusement and perhaps a touch of mischief. "I have been communicating with the spirit world for many years. It is my life's calling, you see. I have helped countless individuals find closure and solace, guiding them through the veil that separates our world from the next. I am quite confident in my abilities. The spirits and I, we have an understanding, a connection that transcends the boundaries of the physical realm."

Quentin said, "Madam Rosalind is truly gifted, Mr Holmes. Her insights have been invaluable to me." He glanced towards the enigmatic woman, admiration in his eyes.

Holmes' gaze focused intently on Madam Rosalind, searching for any tell-tale signs of deception or trickery.

But the medium met his scrutiny with an unflinching stare, her striking green eyes sparkling with amusement and perhaps a touch of defiance.

"The séance will be held tomorrow," she announced. "You and Dr Watson are welcome to attend, of course. But I must warn you, Mr Holmes, to leave any scepticism or negative energy at the door. The spirits can be sensitive to such vibrations." Her words hung in the air, a gentle admonition and a challenge all at once, as if daring the great detective to step into her world of the supernatural.

Watson said, "We wouldn't miss it for the world, would we, Holmes?"

Holmes replied, "We certainly wouldn't."

Madam Rosalind smiled enigmatically. "I look forward to seeing you there, gentlemen. I have a feeling it will be a most enlightening experience."

With a swish of her robes, she turned to Quentin. "Quentin, my dear, I must take my leave. But remember, your future is bright. Embrace your renewed passion, and let nothing hold you back."

Quentin bowed his head. "Thank you, Madam Rosalind. Your words mean the world to me."

As Madam Rosalind glided out of the room, Holmes watched her go, his face holding no expression. When he heard her footsteps become quieter, he said to Quentin Silverstone, "So, how precisely did Madam Rosalind bring about a change in you?"

Quentin began to recount his encounter with Madam Rosalind. "It all began about a month ago. That's when my performance began to slip. I kept forgetting my tricks and which props I should be using. The laughter from the audience, and my fellow performers only made matters worse. This went on for a few nights, my act becoming even more lacklustre. Madam Rosalind visited me here after one of my worst failures and said she could help. I thought I was past all help, but there was something about her that made me listen to her words. She explained how she could put me in a hypnotic state and get to the bottom of what was affecting my career, and once she'd done that, we could work on improving matters.

"She started that night and put me in a trance. Her voice was so hypnotic, I fell asleep within seconds! When I woke up, Madam Rosalind said my ancestors had spoken to her during my trance. They were worried about me and said I had lost my confidence. They said I had a lot of mental blocks that were holding me back from success. It all seemed far-fetched to me, but Madam Rosalind soon convinced me it was true. She said she would need to have more sessions with me, and one day, we would solve my lack of confidence."

Holmes interjected, "And how much did she charge for these visits?"

"Why, nothing at all, Mr Holmes. She said the spirits had led her to me and said it was her moral duty to help me. Which she was more than happy to do." Quentin smiled. "I started looking forward to her visits. She has the most calming of personalities, and her voice when she put me in a trance, oh, it was the voice of an angel. I must admit, I fell asleep every time, so I've no idea what conversations she was having with my ancestors."

"Did you see a change in your performance straight away?" Watson asked. "After Madam Rosalind's first visit?"

Quentin frowned. "I didn't. In fact, things got even worse. I was angry all the time. Angry at myself, at my colleagues, and especially angry at Mr Chamberlain for removing my wax figure. I asked Madam Rosalind why I wasn't feeling better. She explained that my inner doubts were blocking me, keeping me from the success I truly desired. And the more I fought it, the worse it would become. I trusted her, and knew that despite my regular outbursts, there was light at the end of the tunnel."

"And when did that light appear?" Holmes asked with a barely perceptible hint of irony.

"It was yesterday. Mr Barclay had told me a few days ago he was letting me go. I tried to stay optimistic, but when I saw Madam Rosalind waiting for me after my performance yesterday, I told her not to bother trying to help me anymore. But she took my hands and danced me around the room. She said the spirits had spoken to her during my performance and the block in my mind would be lifted during my next trance. She assured me it would be my last trance, and then, I would be cured. I had nothing to lose, so I agreed to one last session. And Madam Rosalind was right! When I woke up from my hypnotic state yesterday, I felt a change inside me. I felt confident, sure of myself. Well, you saw my performance this evening. I am cured. And it's all thanks to Madam Rosalind."

Watson seemed at a loss for words.

But Holmes had something to say, "Mr Silverstone, let me clarify something. When you were in a hypnotic state, could you hear Madam Rosalind at all?"

"No, not a word. But whatever she was saying to the spirits obviously worked. You're a lucky chap to have Madam Rosalind helping you with that mystery of yours. She'll have the spirits sorted out in no time at all! She's amazing." Quentin sighed softly and a wistful look came into his eyes.

"So, let me get this straight," Holmes began. "Madam Rosalind's visits to you were purely to help you overcome any mental blocks you had."

"That's right," Quentin confirmed.

"And she didn't receive any benefit herself, of any kind?" Holmes persisted. "She didn't have an ulterior motive?"

Quentin frowned. "None at all. She helped me because she has a kind heart. And because the spirits told her to."

Holmes' gaze swept around the room, taking in every detail. His eyes fell upon a red box half hidden beneath a dresser. He gestured towards it. "What do you keep in that box, Mr Silverstone?"

Quentin's expression grew serious. "That's where I keep my book of magic tricks. It's my most prized possession, and I never let anyone touch it. It's got details of my performances in it, including regular tricks and ideas for new ones."

"And when did you last look at your book?" Holmes asked.

Quentin considered the question. "Not for a while now. I usually make notes for new illusions after every performance, but since my act started to decline, I didn't have any new ideas to record."

Holmes said, "I wonder if we could look at your book? Not the inside pages, of course, but just to satisfy my curiosity about something. If you don't mind?"

"I don't mind at all." Quentin went over to the dresser. He pulled the box out, and with a few pushes on certain areas, a click sounded out and the box opened. Quentin peered inside it. A frown creased his brow as he reached in and pulled out the book.

"That's strange," he muttered, turning the book over in his hands. "I always place the cover face down, it's a superstition of mine. But just now, it was facing up. Someone has touched it and placed it the wrong way up. Who would do such a thing?"

Holmes stood up and said, "We will leave that mystery to you, at least for the time being. Thank you for talking to us, Mr Silverstone. You have helped us immensely."

With a nod of farewell, Holmes and Watson left the befuddled magician alone with his book of tricks.

# Chapter 16

Holmes and Watson arrived back at 221B Baker Street, both deep in thoughts about the peculiar case they had found themselves embroiled in. As they ascended the stairs to their rooms, Mrs Hudson emerged from her quarters, a telegram in her hand.

"Mr Holmes, Dr Watson," she greeted them, "a telegram arrived for you just a short while ago."

"Thank you, Mrs Hudson," Holmes said, taking the telegram from her. He opened it and quickly scanned the contents.

"It's from Alfred Chamberlain," he informed Watson. "He's confirming that the séance with Madam Rosalind will be held tomorrow evening, after the museum has closed to the public. He formally requests our presence."

Watson gave his friend a considered look. "Holmes, I know how strongly you oppose such things. If you'd prefer, I could attend alone."

Holmes shook his head. "No, no, Watson. I appreciate the offer, but I must be there. I'm interested to see the performance that Madam Rosalind will put on. And I'm sure it will be quite a performance, intended to impress those who are present."

They entered the living room. The fire crackled in the hearth, casting a warm glow over the cluttered space.

Mrs Hudson followed them in. "I'll bring up some dinner for you, gentlemen. You must be famished after your day's adventures."

"That would be most appreciated, Mrs Hudson," Watson said with a smile.

As Mrs Hudson bustled out, Holmes settled into his armchair. Watson took his usual seat opposite him.

"So, what do you make of it all, Holmes?" Watson asked.

Holmes' eyes glinted in the firelight. "There are several threads to this case, Watson, and I'm not yet sure how they all tie together. But I have my suspicions."

"Do you think Marcus Bramwell could be behind the strange occurrences at the museum? He certainly seems to have a motive."

"Indeed, he does," Holmes agreed. "He would undoubtedly benefit from the downfall of Chamberlain's Waxworks. But there's more to it than that. I'm certain he holds other information that could help us. I'm determined to uncover what that is."

Mrs Hudson returned with a tray laden with steaming dishes. She put it on the table and began to lay out the plates.

"What about Thomas Hargreaves?" Watson asked. "Why would he lie to us about his feelings towards Chamberlain?"

Holmes drummed his fingers on the armrest. "That's a question I intend to ask him directly. Again, there's something he's not telling us. Something that could be useful to us."

Mrs Hudson informed them their meal was ready. She left them to it and walked out of the room.

Holmes and Watson sat in their usual seats at the dining table and filled their plates with delicious food.

They ate in contemplative silence for a few minutes, the only sounds the clink of cutlery and the occasional pop from the fire.

"And then there's Madam Rosalind," Holmes said at last. "Her involvement in this case is most curious."

Watson nodded. "It does seem rather convenient that she's holding a séance at the museum just as these hauntings are escalating as if she knew Mr Chamberlain was reaching the end of his tether with them."

"Precisely," Holmes said. "And her connection to Quentin Silverstone adds another layer of intrigue. Why did she contact him out of the blue like that? I don't believe her story about the spirits guiding her to the magician. Why should she care about such a man if there was no benefit to her? She is running a business, after all, and not a charity. She strikes me as a woman who will stop at nothing until she achieves whatever goal she has set for herself."

"And you think her goal is fame and fortune, as you mentioned to Mr Chamberlain earlier?"

"I do," Holmes confirmed. "I suspect Madam Rosalind may have contacted Quentin because she knew about his book of tricks. Perhaps she needed to add more illusions to her own arsenal of tricks. But, of course, asking Quentin outright wouldn't get her that information. You saw how guarded he was when we asked him to reveal how some tricks were done. So, I think she put him into a light trance whilst she contacted those so-called spirits. And while he was in such a relaxed state, or fast asleep as it turned out, she found that red box and unlocked it. Maybe she got Quentin to explain how to open it during one of his trance-like states. She could have made notes about certain tricks, ones she could use in her work. We may very well see some of those tricks tomorrow at the séance. Her mistake was placing the book the wrong way up when returning it to the box."

Watson said, "Quentin told us how someone could create those supposed supernatural conditions at the museum. Whilst he was in a trance, perhaps he told Madam Rosalind, too. And that's how she produced those spooky effects in Mr Chamberlain's building."

Holmes smiled. "That's exactly what I was thinking."

"So, what's our next move, Holmes?"

Holmes replied, "For now, we wait. Tomorrow evening, we'll attend this séance and see what Madam Rosalind has in store. But I have a feeling that the truth will be far more earthly than spiritual."

# Chapter 17

The following afternoon, there was a visitor to 221B Baker Street. Fortunately, Holmes and Watson were both at home to receive her.

Their visitor was Mrs Eliza Morton, the cleaner at Chamberlain's Waxwork Museum. As Mrs Hudson ushered Eliza in, Holmes immediately noticed Mrs Morton's trembling hands and the worry etched on her face.

Holmes rose from his chair. "Mrs Morton. Good afternoon. Please, do take a seat. Mrs Hudson, some tea would be most appreciated."

"Of course, Mr Holmes," Mrs Hudson replied. "I'll bring up a fresh pot and some of that cake I just baked."

Mrs Hudson left the room and Holmes returned to his seated position. He smiled gently at Eliza and said, "Now, Mrs Morton, please tell us what brings you here. Forgive me for saying so, but you seem upset. Can you tell us why?"

Eliza let out a heavy sigh. "Oh, Mr Holmes, Dr Watson, it's the museum. The strange occurrences, they've become worse, much worse. Earlier this morning, some people reported being pushed by invisible hands. One of them stumbled to the floor and injured themselves. And that's not all. There have been voices, too. Whispers in empty rooms, laughter echoing down the halls. And threats. Vile threats hurled at people who walked past the waxworks figures. I could hear complaints coming from all directions. Some people were angry, but a lot of them sounded terrified and I heard them say they would never come back to the museum." She looked down at her hands, twisting them nervously.

Holmes said, "Please, go on, Mrs Morton. If it's not too distressing for you."

Eliza looked up. "Some visitors even claimed to have seen ghostly figures. Apparitions that vanished as quickly as they appeared. I think I might have seen something, too. Just out of the corner of my eye. But I'm sure it's just because everyone's talking about seeing such things. I can't be certain of what I saw, and my mind could be playing tricks on me. One thing I know for certain, is that there is an awful atmosphere amongst the rest of the staff. It's like everyone is on edge, waiting for something terrible to happen. I can't bear it, really I can't."

Mrs Hudson returned with the tea and cake, setting the tray down on the table. She poured each of them a cup before quietly leaving the room.

"Is there anything else, Mrs Morton?" Holmes asked.

Eliza hesitated, then nodded. "Yes, there is. Madam Rosalind arrived after lunchtime. I overheard her talking to Mr Chamberlain when I was doing some cleaning. He told her about the increased activity, and she said something that chilled me to the bone."

Watson asked, "What did she say?"

"She looked straight into Mr Chamberlain's eyes and said the spirits had somehow sensed she was coming to do a séance later. And because they know she will force them to leave the museum, they are causing as much mischief as they can before that happens."

Holmes' eyes narrowed. "And how did Mr Chamberlain react to this?"

Eliza shook her head, a look of unease crossing her face. "That's the strange part. I thought he might dismiss her comments, like he has done before whenever someone mentions spirits and the suchlike to him. But Mr Chamberlain agreed with her wholeheartedly. He said he was glad she was there, and he knew she would rid his museum of spirits. There was something about the way he stared into her eyes. It was unsettling, like he was being hypnotised by her. I didn't like it, Mr Holmes, not one little bit."

Holmes said, "Perhaps Mr Chamberlain was trying to keep Madam Rosalind happy to ensure the séance goes ahead."

Eliza pursed her lips, a look of disgust on her face. "I don't like the idea of a séance. I don't know why there has to be one. Mr Chamberlain said I could watch it, but I won't be there, oh no. I don't like things like that. And there's something about Madam Rosalind that gives me the shivers." She abruptly stopped talking, her lips pressed together as if holding back words.

Holmes gently encouraged her, "Please, Mrs Morton, speak your mind. Whatever it is, it might be important."

With some difficulty, Eliza continued, "After Madam Rosalind finished talking to Mr Chamberlain, he went back to his office. And then, Madam Rosalind turned around and stared right into my eyes, even though I was across the room and thought I hadn't been seen. She came over to me and said she had a message from my late husband, Charlie. She said he was in spirit form and had talked to her."

At the mention of her husband, Eliza's eyes glistened with unshed tears. Dr Watson immediately reached into his pocket and handed her a pressed handkerchief. Eliza accepted it gratefully, dabbing at her eyes.

In a gentle tone, Holmes asked, "What was the message, Mrs Morton?"

Eliza took a deep breath to steady herself. "Charlie's message was, 'Keep away from Sherlock Holmes. He can't be trusted.'"

A heavy silence fell over the room. Holmes and Watson exchanged a glance, both processing the implications of this supposed message from beyond the grave.

Holmes broke the silence, his tone still calm. "Mrs Morton, I assure you that I can be trusted. As can Dr Watson. We have no intention of causing any harm or distress to you or anyone else involved in this case."

Eliza looked up at him, her eyes searching his face. "I know that, Mr Holmes. I don't believe what Madam Rosalind said, not one little bit. Charlie would never say such a thing about you. He admired your work greatly. I'm sure she only said that to scare me. Someone must have told her my husband's name and that he had passed away. But to use that information to unsettle me! It's wicked, it is."

Watson spoke, his voice filled with concern. "Mrs Morton, do you think Madam Rosalind might be involved in these strange occurrences at the museum?"

Eliza hesitated, then nodded slowly. "I don't know for certain, Dr Watson, but I have a feeling she might be. The timing of her arrival today, and the increase in activity before this séance of hers, seems too coincidental."

Holmes nodded. "Your instincts may well be correct, Mrs Morton. Madam Rosalind's actions and words certainly raise suspicions. Watson and I will attend this séance tonight. It will provide an opportunity to observe Madam Rosalind closely and perhaps shed some light on her true intentions."

Watson agreed, "Yes, and we will also keep a close eye on Mr Chamberlain. His behaviour towards Madam Rosalind sounds most peculiar."

Holmes turned to Eliza. "Mrs Morton, I must ask you to be cautious. If Madam Rosalind suspects that you have shared your concerns with us, she may see you as a threat."

Eliza squared her shoulders, a determined look in her eyes. "I understand, Mr Holmes. I'll be careful. But I won't let her intimidate me. I want to help you in any way I can."

Holmes smiled, admiring her courage. "Your assistance is greatly appreciated, Mrs Morton. Please, if you notice anything else unusual, do not hesitate to contact us. Do take care of yourself, especially around Madam Rosalind. Will you stay to finish your tea and cake?"

Eliza stood up. "No, thank you, Mr Holmes. I haven't much of an appetite since Madam Rosalind spoke to me. I'd best be getting back to the museum. If I hear or see anything else, I'll come right back here."

With a final nod and a grateful smile, Eliza left the room, leaving Holmes and Watson to ponder the new information she had provided.

# Chapter 18

As the evening drew near, Holmes and Watson made their way to Chamberlain's Waxwork Museum to attend the séance. When their hansom cab drew up outside the museum, they were amazed to see that the entrance was abuzz with activity as elegantly dressed guests arrived and went inside.

Holmes remarked to his companion that the affair appeared to be more of a societal event than the small gathering he was expecting.

Stepping inside, Holmes and Watson found themselves amidst a crowd of people adorned in their finest attire. The room hummed with excited chatter as the guests speculated about the upcoming event. Among the attendees, a few journalists stood out, their notebooks at the ready, hoping to capture a spectacular story for their papers.

Holmes and Watson made their way through the crowd, alert to the various conversations around them.

A well-dressed elderly woman remarked to her companion, "I attended one of Madam Rosalind's séances last month. It was simply extraordinary! She communicated with the spirits and brought such peace to those in attendance." Her eyes sparkled with excitement as she recounted the experience, her voice filled with reverence for the medium's abilities.

Her friend nodded in agreement. "I've heard similar stories. Madam Rosalind's gift is truly remarkable. I had a private reading with her, and the messages she conveyed from my dear departed mother brought me immense comfort. It was like Mother was right there in the room with us, speaking through her."

In a low voice, Watson said to Holmes, "It seems Madam Rosalind has quite a reputation among the upper echelons of society. Her supposed abilities have garnered her a devoted following."

Holmes inclined his head in agreement. "Yes, but we mustn't accept their accounts without reservation. Perhaps Madam Rosalind requested their presence, knowing she could rely on their unwavering support, regardless of the séance's outcome. She already has the cards stacked in her favour."

Watson smiled at his friend. "Not entirely, Holmes. We are true sceptics of all things paranormal. Madam Rosalind will never convince us that this museum is haunted."

As they continued to mingle, a sudden hush fell over the room. All eyes turned towards the entrance.

Madam Rosalind made her grand appearance. She was a vision in a stunning navy silk dress; the fabric adorned with delicate silver sequins that caught the light with every movement. On her arm, Mr Alfred Chamberlain stood tall, his eyes locked adoringly on Madam Rosalind's face.

Holmes' keen gaze observed the interaction between the two. He leaned closer to Watson and whispered, "Mr Chamberlain appears to be completely under Madam Rosalind's spell. This could prove problematic for our investigation."

Watson took in the scene. "You're right, Holmes. There's an unsettling dynamic at play here."

Madam Rosalind and Mr Chamberlain made their way through the crowd, acknowledging the guests with graceful nods and charming smiles.

Madam Rosalind cast a gracious smile on the people before her, her gaze resting for a moment on Holmes. Lifting her chin, she announced, "The séance is about to begin.

Please, follow me and I will lead you to the most haunted part of this building where the séance will take place."

A murmur of anticipation ran through the gathered people.

Under his breath, Watson said, "I hope it's not that reconstructed street. I'm in no mood to see Jack the Ripper pouncing out of the shadows."

Holmes smiled at his comments. "Let's see where Madam Rosalind takes us."

Madam Rosalind led the guests into the large room where waxwork figures of royalty and famous historic figures stood on raised platforms.

Watson leaned closer to Holmes and said, "I'm surprised the séance will take place here. I didn't think this was the most haunted area, at least not to me."

Holmes nodded, his brow furrowed in thought. "There's something 'off' about this room, Watson. Something I felt yesterday when we were here. But for the life of me, I can't quite put my finger on it."

A large table had been placed in the centre of the room, draped in a purple velvet cloth and surrounded by eight chairs. Three rows of additional chairs were arranged in a circle around the table, providing seating for those not invited to sit at the main table itself.

The journalists eagerly made their way to the front row, their pens poised and ready to capture every detail of the impending event.

Madam Rosalind gracefully took her seat at the head of the table, while Mr Chamberlain positioned himself opposite her. Holmes and Watson were about to settle into the outer row of chairs near the back of the room when Madam Rosalind's voice rang out across the room.

"Mr Holmes, Dr Watson, I must insist that you join me at this table. I would like you on either side of me. I politely ask that you don't bring your usual scepticism and non-belief about the spirit realms with you. Your negative feelings will affect my energy." A smug smile played on her lips as she said to the rest of the room, "I will convince the famous Sherlock Holmes and Dr Watson that spirits do, indeed, exist. By the end of this evening, I shall turn them from sceptics into believers."

Holmes and Watson had no choice but to comply with Madam Rosalind's request. They made their way to the table and took their seats on either side of her, their discomfort evident in their expressions.

Madam Rosalind, on the other hand, seemed to revel in their unease. She gave them a satisfied smile, her eyes glinting with a hint of triumph.

Once everyone was seated, Madam Rosalind said, "The séance shall now commence. From now on, the only voices you will hear will be mine and those of the visiting spirits."

# Chapter 19

Madam Rosalind closed her eyes, her head tilted back slightly as if listening to a distant voice.

"Let us join hands," she intoned, her voice low and melodic. "We must create an unbroken circle, a conduit for the spirits to reach us."

Holmes and Watson exchanged a sceptical glance but did as instructed. They clasped hands with Madam Rosalind and the others seated at the table, forming a chain of linked fingers.

Madam Rosalind took a deep breath, the air seeming to crackle with anticipation. "Spirits of the beyond," she called out, her voice resonating through the room, "we implore you to make your presence known. Speak to us, guide us, and share your wisdom from the other side."

A gust of cold wind swept through the room, causing the candle flames to flicker and dance. The journalists in the front row leaned forward, their notepads open, ready to record every detail.

"I sense a presence," Madam Rosalind whispered, her brow furrowed in concentration. "A restless soul, trapped within these walls, yearning to be heard."

Some low gasps came from several areas.

Suddenly, a loud knock echoed through the room, causing several people to gasp. Madam Rosalind's eyes flew open, her gaze intense and focused.

"The spirits are among us," she declared, her voice trembling with emotion. "They wish to communicate."

Another knock, this time more insistent, reverberated through the space. The waxwork figures seemed to loom larger, their eyes gleaming in the candlelight.

Madam Rosalind began to speak, her words flowing in a stream of cryptic messages. "The past and the present collide, secrets buried deep within these walls. A betrayal, a hidden truth, a score to settle."

The room grew colder and strange shadows flickered across the walls, some of them eerily human-like.

Madam Rosalind's voice rose in pitch, her words becoming more urgent. "The spirits demand justice, a wrong to be righted. The truth must be revealed, or the haunting will continue."

Suddenly, a gust of wind extinguished the candles, plunging the room into darkness. Gasps and murmurs filled the air as the guests grappled with the sudden blackness. Ghostly groans and moans filled the air.

In the midst of the confusion, a piercing scream rang out, followed by the sound of shattering glass. Some people cried out in fear.

Holmes and Watson leapt to their feet.

"Remain calm!" Holmes called out, his voice cutting through the panic. "Watson, find a light source!"

As Watson fumbled in the darkness, a faint glow began to emanate from the centre of the table. Slowly, the light grew brighter, revealing Madam Rosalind, her eyes closed and her face contorted in a trance-like state.

The room fell silent, all eyes fixated on the eerie spectacle before them.

Watson reignited the candles and returned to his seated position. Holmes did the same, his steely glance focused on Madam Rosalind as he wondered what she was going to do next.

Madam Rosalind, her voice now a haunting whisper, spoke once more. "The spirits attached to these waxworks have sent me a message," she intoned, her eyes still closed in a trance-like state. "They are upset because of the fear and confusion they have caused. They only wished to make their presence known, to greet the visitors of the museum. They never wished to cause any harm." She nodded, as if receiving a new message. "Ah, yes, thank you. The spirits would like to give their appreciation to the owner of this museum, who set forth the process of creating them. They say he has done an excellent job and they are most impressed."

Holmes' gaze shifted to Chamberlain, noting the proud look that appeared on the man's face. It was a curious reaction, given the eerie circumstances that surrounded them.

Madam Rosalind said, "Spirits, thank you for talking to me. I appreciate your concerns, but I respectfully ask you to leave this building; to leave it in peace. Thank you, kind spirits, thank you."

A series of low groans came from the waxwork figures, followed by shadows racing across the room; shadows that vanished a few seconds later.

Holmes wondered how Madam Rosalind had created such illusions. He had to admit, they were extremely effective.

Suddenly, the atmosphere shifted, and a sense of unease permeated the air. Madam Rosalind's brow furrowed, and her voice took on a sharper edge. "An angry spirit is trying to get my attention. Spirit, yes, I can hear you. Spirit, please do not curse! Tell me what angers you so. Ah, I see. Yes, I do understand. We are of the same mind. Yes, I will tell them." She opened her eyes and said, "The spirit is upset with certain people in this room; people who doubt the existence of the spiritual world beyond the veil. The spirit has heard the way these two men talk about such matters, and it has ignited a fury in him. He wants these men to leave the museum and never set foot in it again."

Holmes could feel the weight of eyes upon him, but he didn't say a word. Watson squirmed in his seat, trying to avoid looking left or right at those who were glowering at him.

Madam Rosalind smiled, her gaze sweeping across the room. "The spirits have departed," she announced, her voice clear and strong. "The museum is now free from their presence."

A murmur of relief and amazement rippled through the assembled guests. Some of them broke into a round of applause. The journalists scribbled furiously in their notebooks.

As people began to leave the room, Madam Rosalind sank back in her chair, a look of satisfaction and exhaustion etched upon her face.

Mr Chamberlain rushed to Madam Rosalind's side, his face a picture of concern. "Madam Rosalind, are you all right?" he asked, his voice tinged with worry.

She smiled up at him. "Contacting the spirit world always takes its toll, Mr Chamberlain," she replied. "But I assure you, the spiritual activity that has plagued your museum will cease from this moment forward."

Chamberlain's face broke into a wide smile, his admiration for Madam Rosalind evident in his expression. "I cannot thank you enough, Madam Rosalind," he gushed, taking her hand in his. "I should have accepted your offer of assistance the moment you reached out to me. It was foolish of me to delay matters."

Madam Rosalind inclined her head graciously, accepting his praise. However, her gaze soon drifted past Chamberlain, settling on Holmes, who was still sitting at her side.

Chamberlain, noticing the shift in Madam Rosalind's attention, turned brusquely to face Holmes and Watson. "Gentlemen," he said, his tone curt and dismissive, "it appears that your services are no longer required. With all due respect, I must ask you to leave the museum immediately."

Holmes raised an eyebrow, his expression unreadable. Watson, however, looked taken aback by the sudden change in Chamberlain's demeanour.

"Please send your bill for any services rendered thus far," Chamberlain continued, waving a hand dismissively. "But consider this matter closed. Madam Rosalind has resolved the situation, and there is no further need for your involvement. And you heard what that angry spirit said to this dear woman. It's clear he was talking about you and Dr Watson as the ones who had vexed him. I can't take the chance of him returning and causing trouble."

Holmes' gaze locked with Madam Rosalind's for a brief moment, noticing the glimmer of triumph in her eyes.

Then, with a slight nod, he turned to Watson. "Come, Watson," he said quietly. "It appears our presence is no longer welcome."

Once outside the museum, Watson turned to Holmes, his face a mixture of confusion and frustration. "Holmes, what just happened in there?" he asked, gesturing back towards the museum. "Do you believe Madam Rosalind truly communicated with spirits, or was it all an elaborate hoax? I must say, she was very convincing. It was quite a show she put on."

"It was a show, my dear Watson, an extremely elaborate show. She wasn't communicating with the other world, but I wondered if she was communicating with us in some way."

Watson gave him a confused look. "I don't understand. Did I miss something?"

Holmes said, "At the beginning of the séance, Madam Rosalind mentioned a betrayal, a score that needed to be settled. She said there were secrets deep within the walls of the building. She never explained what those words meant, or if they were intended for anyone in particular."

Watson nodded. "I see. Do you think she has been betrayed by Mr Chamberlain or one of his employees in the past? Or do her words have something to do with this building and what may have happened here?"

"I'm note sure," Holmes replied. "Those words struck me as odd. I was going to speak to her about those comments, but alas, thanks to her clever invention of a vengeful spirit who has taken against us, that conversation won't take place. I must admit, I wasn't impressed with how quickly she dismissed the so-called spirits from the museum, or the reasons why she claimed they were causing mischief. Far too simple and not at all entertaining, in my opinion. I was expecting a lot more from Madam Rosalind, going by how popular she is. Yet, she achieved her purpose. I'm sure the newspapers will be full of her antics tomorrow. And Mr Chamberlain is certain the strange activities have now stopped."

Watson said, "What do you propose we do now?" he asked, falling into step beside Holmes as they walked away from the museum.

Holmes sighed. "There's nothing more we can do at the moment. We have been dismissed by Mr Chamberlain. But I have a feeling that this mystery is far from over."

# Chapter 20

Over the next week, Holmes and Watson put the events of the séance behind them, focusing their attention on the new cases that arrived at their doorstep. One particularly intriguing case involved a missing heirloom, a family feud, and a web of deceit that kept the duo busy for several days. Another case, brought to them by a distressed young lady, revolved around a series of anonymous letters that threatened to expose a scandalous secret from her past.

One afternoon, upon the completion of their latest case, Holmes and Watson decided to take advantage of the fine weather and take a walk outside. They hadn't got very far, when they saw someone familiar heading towards them. It was Marcus Bramwell, smiling from ear to ear, and tipping his hat at every woman who passed him.

"He certainly looks pleased with himself," Watson noted. "I thought he would be annoyed about things turning around for Mr Chamberlain following that séance. After all, there's no chance of him buying the museum now."

"Yes, he does seem suspiciously chipper," Holmes agreed.

Mr Bramwell spotted them and called out, "Mr Holmes! Dr Watson! What a pleasure to see you. Isn't it a most splendid day?" He stopped in front of them, clearly wanting to engage them in conversation.

Holmes said, "Good afternoon, Mr Bramwell. You seem in fine spirits. May I ask, is there a reason for that?"

"Oh, absolutely!" His voice brimmed with delight. "I am positively thrilled about the recent turn of events at the Chamberlain Waxwork Museum."

Holmes and Watson exchanged puzzled glances.

"I beg your pardon, Mr Bramwell," Holmes said. "The last we heard, the museum was thriving after Madam Rosalind's supposed banishment of the spirits. Has something changed?"

Bramwell let out a hearty laugh, his eyes twinkling with amusement. "Oh, my dear Mr Holmes, there have been some rather interesting developments just this morning. While I don't have all the details, I do know that Her Majesty, Queen Victoria, was scheduled to visit the museum this morning. The establishment was closed to the general public for the occasion. But that's not the most intriguing part. Just after lunch, I was strolled past the museum. I noticed a sign indicating that the museum had been closed permanently with immediate effect."

"Closed? Just like that?" Holmes pressed.

Bramwell's eyes glinted with joy. "That's not all, gentlemen. I heard a rumour from a friend that Mr Chamberlain has been arrested by the police. Something about an incident during the Queen's visit, and there are whispers of 'treason' floating about. He is presently locked up behind bars at the local prison."

Watson asked, "But what exactly happened during the Queen's visit?"

"I've no idea," Bramwell replied. "And I don't much care. All I know is that the museum building will be up for sale soon, and I fully intend to make it mine. Good day to you both."

As Bramwell walked away, Holmes turned to Watson, his expression grave. "We must head to the prison immediately, Watson," he declared. "We need to find out what happened during the Queen's visit and why Chamberlain has been arrested."

Watson nodded in agreement. "Of course, Holmes. But treason? Against the Queen herself? I can scarcely believe it."

Holmes said, "I truly hope Madam Rosalind isn't behind this, but I wouldn't be surprised if she were. Despite being dismissed by him, I hope Mr Chamberlain will speak to us. I have a feeling he needs us now more than ever."

# Chapter 21

The prison loomed before Holmes and Watson, its grey stone walls and barred windows a stark reminder of the grim fate that had befallen Mr Chamberlain. As they entered the dank, dimly lit building, the echoes of their footsteps mingled with the distant sounds of clanging metal doors and the muffled cries of inmates.

A guard, his face weathered and his eyes weary from years of service, led them through a maze of narrow corridors, past cells filled with despondent faces and hollow eyes. The prisoners, some resigned to their fate and others still clinging to a faint glimmer of hope, watched as the unlikely pair passed by, their presence a fleeting distraction from the monotony of incarceration.

At last, they reached the cell where Mr Chamberlain was being held. The once-proud owner of the waxwork museum sat hunched on a narrow cot, his face gaunt and his eyes ringed with dark circles, a shadow of the jovial man he had been mere days before. He looked up as Holmes and Watson approached, a flicker of relief crossing his features.

"Mr Holmes, Dr Watson," Chamberlain said. "I can't tell you how pleased I am to see you. I asked if I could send you a telegram requesting your presence, but was told no. But here you are. How did you know where to find me?"

Holmes answered, "Mr Bramwell told us about your predicament."

"Pah!" Chamberlain exclaimed. "I can imagine how happy that made him. But I'm grateful he did, because his words led you here. I am hoping with all my heart that you are here to help me. Although, I have no right to ask for your help, not after the way I treated you at the séance. You have my sincere apologies for the terrible way I spoke to you."

Holmes waved away the apology with a dismissive gesture of his hand. "You did what you thought was best at the time, Mr Chamberlain. We are here to offer our services, if you would like us to."

Chamberlain sagged in relief. "Thank you, Mr Holmes, Dr Watson. My situation is dire, very dire, indeed."

Dr Watson said, "Marcus Bramwell told us you had been arrested, and that 'treason' was the reason why. Surely, that's not the case."

Chamberlain gave them a grim-faced nod. "Alas, Dr Watson. It is true."

"Tell us everything," Holmes advised.

Chamberlain explained, "Following the newspaper article about Madam Rosalind's séance. Oh, did you see the papers?"

Holmes said, "I only saw the headline. 'Madam Rosalind Succeeds Where Sherlock Holmes Fails'. Please, continue."

Chamberlain cleared his throat, obviously embarrassed by the news headline. "Yes, right. After the séance, I received a message straight from the Palace. It was from Queen Victoria. She had seen the newspaper and wanted to see the museum for herself. She mentioned she had an interest in the paranormal and would love to know more about what had happened there during the séance."

"Did the Queen ask that Madam Rosalind be present at her visit?" Holmes asked.

Chamberlain shook his head. "I was glad about that as I never want to see Madam Rosalind ever again. I should have trusted you, Mr Holmes. You were right to be wary of her, and her so-called abilities. I allowed myself to be taken in by Madam Rosalind's charms, to believe that there was a special connection between us, something beyond the mundane world. I see now that I was merely a pawn in her game, a means to an end."

Watson said, "What happened, Mr Chamberlain? What made you realise that Madam Rosalind was not what she seemed?"

Chamberlain sighed heavily, his hand passing over his weary face as he recounted the painful memory. "A few days after the séance, I called at her house, hoping to invite her to dinner. I had thought, perhaps foolishly, that there was a genuine connection between us. But when I arrived, I saw the contempt in her eyes, and I heard the disdain in her voice. She told me, in no uncertain terms, that I was far too old for her, that I had misread the situation entirely. I was nothing more than a gullible old man to her.

"But that wasn't all. As I was leaving, dejected and humiliated, I noticed another room in her house, filled with people waiting for private readings. They were all eagerly anticipating their turn with the great Madam Rosalind." A note of bitterness crept into his voice. "And everywhere I looked, there were copies of newspapers, all praising Madam Rosalind's incredible abilities, her gift for communing with the spirits. It was then that I realised the true extent of her deception. It was just as you predicted, Mr Holmes, all Madam Rosalind is interested in is fame and fortune. She uses people to achieve those things, and when she has no further use for those people, she discards them without a second thought."

Holmes nodded. "I'm sorry you were so humiliated by her, Mr Chamberlain. She does have a way of easily manipulating others. But, please, tell us more about Queen Victoria's visit."

Chamberlain continued, "Arrangements were made for the Queen to visit the museum this morning. We closed it to the public and ensured the place was spotless. Thomas had just completed the waxwork of Her Majesty and we rushed to put it in place. The figure was the best work Thomas had ever undertaken. It was a work of art. I knew Her Majesty would be impressed. My plan was to show the figure first, and then tell the Queen more about the hauntings and the séance, pushing my feelings about Madam Rosalind to one side, of course.

"But things didn't work out that way. Queen Victoria arrived promptly at ten o'clock, accompanied by her ladies-in-waiting and a small contingent of guards. I greeted her at the entrance and escorted her directly to the room housing her new waxwork figure. I stood to one side to let her enter first. Only seconds later, I heard a gasp followed by an outrage cry. I dashed into the room and saw..." He paused to gather himself. "I saw that the beautiful waxwork figure of Queen Victoria had been sabotaged. Someone had deliberately caused it to melt, leaving a horrendous mess behind."

Dr Watson declared, "Good heavens! What happened then?"

"I tried to placate the Queen, told her someone had caused the damage on purpose to destroy my business. But she wouldn't listen. She demanded that I be arrested on the spot, and that the museum be shut down." He held his hands out helplessly. "And here I am. Ready to await my sentence. I keep thinking about that melted waxwork. It's deliberate sabotage, I'm sure of it. But who would do such a thing?"

Holmes said, "That is what we intend to find out, Mr Chamberlain. You have my word that Watson and I will do everything in our power to uncover the true culprit behind this heinous act. I suspect it could be the same person who has been behind these strange occurrences all along. Whoever it is, they have played an excellent game of deception, weaving a web of lies and misdirection. But I assure you, we shall bring the perpetrator to justice."

Chamberlain's eyes shone with gratitude. "Thank you, Mr Holmes. I don't know what I would do without your help. You have my full permission to access any part of the museum, if that would help. Please, do whatever you must to clear my name and restore the reputation of my beloved museum." He patted his pocket. "Unfortunately, I was rushed out of the museum so quickly that I didn't get the chance to collect my keys. There may be a member of staff still at the museum who could let you in, but I have a feeling everyone has left."

Holmes smiled and said, "I don't need keys. I have a way of opening locked doors. We must take our leave, Mr Chamberlain, but we will return soon, and we will return with good news."

# Chapter 22

Holmes and Watson stepped out of the prison, their minds heavy with the weight of Chamberlain's plight. As they made their way towards the Waxwork Museum, Holmes' keen eyes spotted a familiar figure leaving the building and heading in the direction of the King's Arms pub.

"Watson, look there," Holmes said, pointing discreetly. "It's Thomas Hargreaves, and he seems to be in quite a hurry. I believe it's time we had another chat with Mr Hargreaves, especially in light of what has happened this morning."

The two men followed Hargreaves at a distance, careful not to draw attention to themselves. They entered the pub and found him sitting in a dimly lit corner, a pint of beer already in hand. Holmes and Watson approached his table and took a seat across from him.

Before either of them could speak, Hargreaves raised his glass and smirked. "Well, well, if it isn't the great Sherlock Holmes and his trusty sidekick. Come to drown your sorrows over the museum's closure?"

Holmes said, "On the contrary, Mr Hargreaves. We're here to discuss your role in this whole affair."

Hargreaves scoffed. "My role? I had nothing to do with it. In fact, I'm glad that wretched place is shut down."

Watson exchanged a glance with Holmes before speaking. "When we spoke to you before, you claimed to be happy with your job. Why the sudden change of heart?"

Hargreaves took a long swig of his beer, his eyes darkening. "Happy? That was a load of rubbish. I only said that because I needed the work. But Chamberlain and I didn't get along. He was always demanding more, never satisfied with my efforts. Do you know how many hours I spent slaving away in that workshop, creating his precious waxworks? And what thanks did I get? Nothing but criticism and contempt. Do you remember that waxwork figure I made of Queen Victoria? It was my best work ever. But it's been destroyed. And it's got something to do with Chamberlain. One of his enemies getting revenge, I expect, and my artwork has been mutilated in the process. I didn't deserve that, not at all."

Holmes listened intently, allowing Hargreaves to vent his frustrations. When the sculptor paused to take another sip of beer, Holmes interjected. "Did your resentment drive you to cause the strange occurrences at the museum? The unexplained noises, the moving figures?"

Hargreaves let out a bitter laugh. "I wish I'd been that clever. No, Mr Holmes, I had nothing to do with those happenings. Though I can't say I'm sorry they occurred. Chamberlain deserved every bit of trouble that came his way."

Watson leaned in, his brow furrowed. "What about Madam Rosalind? Do you think she could have been behind it all?"

Hargreaves shook his head. "I doubt it. She's a bit of a charlatan, if you ask me. All that talk of spirits and whatnot. But…" He hesitated, his glance darting around the pub.

Holmes' gaze sharpened. "But what, Mr Hargreaves? If you have information, it's crucial that you share it with us."

Hargreaves sighed, lowering his voice. "Well, I did see her setting up some strange equipment before that séance evening. Wires, pulleys, that sort of thing. Thought it was odd at the time, but I didn't say anything. Figured it was none of my business."

Watson nodded. "We were there at the séance. We saw the illusions she created."

Holmes said, "Mr Hargreaves, during our initial meeting at the museum, you presented yourself as content in your work. Why did you not share your true feelings then?"

"If I had spoken ill of Chamberlain then, he might have overheard. The man has ears everywhere."

Watson frowned, puzzled. "But we were in your workshop, Mr Hargreaves. Surely, you could have spoken freely there?"

Hargreaves leaned forward, his voice lowering to a conspiratorial whisper. "You don't know the half of it. That museum is full of secrets, including passageways that Chamberlain uses to move about unseen. He could have been lurking behind any wall, listening to our every word. I often get the feeling I'm being watched, even when I'm alone in my workshop."

Holmes said, "Secret passageways? I had no idea. This changes things considerably."

Hargreaves nodded, a grim satisfaction on his face. "Oh, yes. Chamberlain is a sly one. Uses those hidden corridors to keep tabs on everyone, making sure we're all toeing the line."

Watson frowned. "But why would he need such a thing? Surely, as the owner, he could go where he pleased?"

"It's not about access, Dr Watson," Hargreaves explained. "It's about control. Chamberlain likes to know everything that goes on in his precious museum, without anyone being the wiser."

Holmes leaned back in his chair. "Mr Hargreaves, this information could be vital to our investigation. Is there any way you could show us these passageways?"

Hargreaves hesitated for a moment, then reached into his pocket and pulled out a set of keys. He slid them across the table to Holmes. "Here, take these. They'll get you into the museum and Chamberlain's office. I won't be needing them anymore, not now that I'm done with that place."

Holmes picked up the keys, examining them closely. "And in his office, we'll find the plans for the building? The ones that reveal the secret passageways?"

Hargreaves nodded. "That's right. Chamberlain keeps them locked up tight, but with those keys, you should be able to get your hands on them."

"How do you know about these passageways, Mr Hargreaves?" Holmes asked.

Hargreaves smirked. "Everyone who works there knows about them. I can't remember who told me, but it's common knowledge amongst the staff. Of course, Chamberlain isn't aware of this. He thinks he's got one over on us, but he hasn't."

Watson looked at Holmes. "This could be the break we've been looking for, Holmes. If Madam Rosalind or someone else has been using these passageways to create the illusion of hauntings..."

"Then we may be closer to unravelling this mystery than we thought," Holmes finished, a glint of determination in his eye. He turned back to Hargreaves. "Thank you, Mr Hargreaves. Your information has been most helpful."

Hargreaves waved a dismissive hand. "Don't mention it. Just promise me one thing, Mr Holmes. When you catch the person responsible for all this, make sure they pay for what they've done. Chamberlain may be a difficult man, but he doesn't deserve to rot in prison for someone else's crimes."

Holmes nodded solemnly. "You have my word, Mr Hargreaves. Justice will be served, one way or another."

With that, Holmes and Watson bid farewell to the disgruntled sculptor and made their way out of the pub. As they stepped into the cool London air, Holmes turned to his companion, a glint of anticipation in his eye.

"Come, Watson. We have a set of plans to examine and a network of secret passageways to explore. We are getting closer to discovering the person who's responsible for all this trouble."

# Chapter 23

Holmes and Watson walked briskly towards Chamberlain's Waxwork Museum. Upon reaching the building, they were greeted by a large sign on the door, proclaiming in bold letters: "CLOSED PERMANENTLY."

Holmes pulled out the set of keys Hargreaves had given them. With a deft turn of the key, the lock on the main door clicked open, and the two men stepped inside the museum. The silence that greeted them was eerie, the usual bustle of visitors replaced by an oppressive stillness.

As they made their way through the exhibits, they came upon the melted figure of Queen Victoria. Watson shook his head, a mixture of disbelief and sympathy on his face.

"The poor Queen," he murmured. "To see herself depicted in such a manner... it must have been quite a shock."

Holmes examined the distorted features of the waxwork. "It's clear that this was no accident. Someone deliberately sabotaged this figure, knowing full well the reaction it would provoke."

They continued on, their footsteps echoing in the empty halls, until they reached Chamberlain's office. Holmes immediately set to work, rifling through drawers and files with practised efficiency. Watson went to the other side of the room to see if he could find anything useful there.

"Aha!" Holmes exclaimed, holding up a set of blueprints. "Here we are, Watson. The plans for the museum. Let's have a good look at them." He opened them out on the table.

Watson hurried over, peering over Holmes' shoulder at the intricate lines and symbols. "Good Lord, Holmes. Those hidden passageways are everywhere. Running behind the walls, connecting the exhibits…"

Holmes traced a finger along one of the passages. "And look here, Watson. A passageway running alongside the room housing King Henry VIII and other royal figures. The very room where I felt something was amiss, remember?"

Watson peered closer. "Of course! That room is smaller than the one preceding it. That must be because the passageway was taking up some of the space. Well spotted, Holmes. I never would have noticed such a thing. That explains all the strange activity in that area. Someone must have caused the incidents from within that hidden area. But how?"

Holmes folded up the plans and tucked them into his coat pocket. "We will soon have the answer to that question. Let us proceed to that place and find a way into the passageway. With some luck and keen observation, we might locate a clue."

Watson nodded, steeling himself for the task ahead. "Lead on then, Holmes. Let's see what secrets these walls have to hide." As soon as he said those last words, his eyes widened. "That's what Madam Rosalind said during her séance, or something similar. That there were secrets deep within the walls of the museum."

Holmes said, "I was about to say the same thing to you, my dear Watson. If she is the culprit, let's see if Madam Rosalind has left any evidence behind."

With that, the two men exited the office and made their way back through the museum. As they approached the room housing the Tudor monarch, Holmes paused, his eyes scanning the walls with intense concentration. He moved over to the wall where the passageway was, according to the blueprints, and ran his hands gently over the patterned wallpaper.

"There," he said, pointing to a barely visible seam in the wallpaper. "That must be the entrance to the passageway. Now, how do I open this door?"

Holmes' nimble fingers probed the edges of the door, searching for a mechanism. After a moment, he pressed firmly on a slightly raised portion of the wall, and with a soft click, the door swung open, revealing a narrow, dimly lit passageway.

"Ingenious," Holmes murmured, stepping inside. "A spring-loaded mechanism, triggered by pressure on a specific point."

Watson followed close behind. They noticed a gas lamp hanging on a nail, its soft light casting eerie shadows on the walls. Holmes reached up and carefully lifted the lamp from its perch, holding it aloft to illuminate their path.

Holmes said, "Someone has left this lamp burning, which suggests there has been a recent visitor to this hallway. Perhaps it's the same person who caused damage to the Queen's waxwork figure."

As they walked, they soon noticed small holes at eye height along the passageway, spaced at regular intervals. Watson peered through one of the holes and gasped. "Holmes, look. You get an excellent view of the room from here."

Holmes peered through another hole, his brow furrowed in concentration. "Yes, and from this vantage point, it's perfect for observing the reactions of unsuspecting visitors. And because of the intricate pattern of the wallpaper on the other side, it would be easy to remain unspotted. Let's examine this area thoroughly. The culprit may have left something behind."

Holmes ran his hand slowly over the wall, searching for evidence.

Watson did the same, and moments later, he said, "Holmes, look at this. There's a nail sticking out here, and on it, is a scrap of fabric."

"Well done, my friend. Please put that in your pocket. That could be the evidence we're looking for. But, on the other hand, it could be nothing significant. Let's keep looking."

"Rightio." Watson took a folded handkerchief from his pocket and carefully placed the fabric inside it. He put the handkerchief back in his pocket, adding a little tap of satisfaction.

They continued searching the area.

Holmes got to his knees. He placed the lamp at his side and ran his hands over the lower part of the wall. All of a sudden, he let out a cry of jubilation.

"What have you found?" Watson asked, kneeling next to him.

Holmes placed his fingers smoothly against the wall. He said, "This area is slightly raised. I am hoping there is a concealed compartment here. Let me see if I can find a way to open it. Maybe it's the same spring mechanism that's on the door."

A click sounded out, and a large drawer slid smoothly open.

Inside the drawer was a variety of items; wires, pulleys and something else.

Holmes picked an item up and examined it more closely. He gave Watson a grim look. "Looks like we've found our culprit."

# Chapter 24

Holmes and Watson sat in their cosy living room at 221B Baker Street, the morning sun streaming through the windows. The room was filled with the aroma of freshly brewed tea and the faint scent of pipe tobacco. Holmes reclined in his armchair, deep in thought. Watson, ever the early riser, sat at the desk, pen in hand, jotting down notes from their latest case.

A soft knock at the door drew their attention. "Come in, Mrs Hudson," Holmes called out.

The door opened, and Mrs Hudson entered, followed by a nervous-looking Mrs Eliza Morton. "Mrs Morton to see you, Mr Holmes," Mrs Hudson announced, a warm smile on her face.

Holmes rose from his chair, a welcoming smile on his lips. "Ah, Mrs Morton, thank you for coming. Please, do take a seat." He gestured towards the settee, his voice gentle and reassuring.

Eliza nodded, her hands clasped tightly in front of her. She made her way to the settee and sat down. "Thank you for seeing me, Mr Holmes, Dr Watson. I hope I'm not interrupting anything important, but your telegram said you wanted to see me as soon as possible. I've never had a telegram before." She gave them a small smile.

Watson put down his pen and moved over to his usual armchair. He said, "I hope the telegram didn't cause you any distress. We invited you here to tell you about our latest case, the one involving the wax museum."

Eliza said, "Have you found out who did it, Dr Watson? I'm ever so worried about Mr Chamberlain, what with him being in prison and all. It's just not right, him being locked up like that."

Holmes nodded, his expression sympathetic. "I understand your concern, Mrs Morton. It's a troubling situation, to be sure."

"And that waxwork of Her Majesty, Queen Victoria," Eliza continued, her voice trembling slightly. "Who would do such a wicked thing, melting it like that? It's just horrible, it is."

Holmes replied, "Indeed, it is a most distressing act of vandalism. But I assure you, Mrs Morton, Dr Watson and I have been working tirelessly to unravel the mystery of the hauntings at the museum. And I am pleased to say that we have solved the case."

Eliza's eyes widened. "You have, Mr Holmes? Oh, that's wonderful news! I knew you'd get to the bottom of it, I did. Is it Madam Rosalind, then? I've had my suspicions about her from the start, what with all her talk of spirits and such."

Holmes shook his head. "No, Mrs Morton, much as it pains me to admit it, Madam Rosalind is not the culprit behind the hauntings. While she certainly staged some of the effects at the séance, likely learned from her association with Quentin Silverstone, she is not responsible for the larger mystery."

Eliza frowned, confusion etched on her face. "Quentin Silverstone? I've never heard of him. Who is he?"

A heavy silence fell. Holmes leaned back in his chair, his eyes fixed on Eliza, who stared at the clock on the mantelpiece.

Finally, Holmes spoke, his voice gentle yet firm. "Mrs Morton, you must know who Quentin Silverstone is. You have been working as a cleaner at the theatre where he performs for the past three years, and you often stop to talk to him in his dressing room when he's resting between performances."

Eliza's eyes widened, her hands clasped tightly in her lap. She opened her mouth as if to speak, but no words came out.

Holmes continued, "After making an interesting discovery at the museum yesterday afternoon, Dr Watson and I called on Quentin last evening. He spoke very fondly of you, Mrs Morton. He mentioned how interested you were in his magic tricks and how he even shared the secrets behind some of his simpler illusions with you. He didn't know you worked at the waxworks museum and was extremely surprised when we told him."

Eliza's cheeks flushed, and she looked down at her hands, her fingers twisting together. The silence stretched on, broken only by the soft ticking of the clock.

"And that's not all," Holmes said, his voice still gentle but with an undercurrent of steel. "You also work as a cleaner at Marcus Bramwell's establishment, don't you? And you're on friendly terms with him as well."

At the mention of Bramwell's name, Eliza slowly smiled. She looked up and said, "Marcus is a wonderful man. He always has time for me, always greets me by name and asks how I am. Not like some places where I'm invisible, where no one even sees me, let alone knows my name. But not Marcus, he always notices me." She stopped talking, a faraway look in her eyes. "He sees me as I am. I'm not invisible to him, not at all."

Holmes continued, "Is that why you created the disturbances at the museum, Mrs Morton? The ones that led to rumours about it being haunted?"

Eliza's eyes widened, her hands gripping the fabric of her skirt. She fell silent again, her lips pressed together in a thin line.

"You knew how Marcus felt betrayed by Alfred Chamberlain," Holmes said. "He had spoken to you about that during one of your chats, hadn't he? And so, you caused the disturbances with the aim of getting the museum to close. Then, Mr Bramwell could buy it."

Eliza's gaze remained fixed on her lap, her shoulders hunched as if under a great weight.

Dr Watson spoke, "We weren't sure why you would create the disturbances, Mrs Morton. At first, we thought you might have a grudge against Mr Chamberlain. Perhaps he had treated you harshly or was critical of your work. But then, Holmes wondered if there was another reason; a score to settle, so to speak. But a score on someone else's behalf which led us to Mr Bramwell. We paid him a visit yesterday, and he told us about your chats."

Eliza looked up, a smile on her face. "He did? He talked about me? He's such a lovely man, don't you think so, Dr Watson? And so very handsome, too."

Dr Watson merely smiled, but gave no response.

Holmes looked at Eliza and said, "You must have been angry with Madam Rosalind and her séance, claiming that the so-called spirits had left. You could have waited a while before starting up the disturbances again. But instead, you resorted to something so shocking, something you knew would cause the museum to be closed immediately."

Eliza averted her gaze.

"You were the one who caused the damage to Queen Victoria's waxwork, weren't you, Mrs Morton?" Holmes' voice was gentle, but there was no mistaking the underlying accusation. "Watson, would you be so kind as to show Mrs Morton what we found inside that hidden passageway at the museum?"

Watson reached towards a box sitting on a table at the side. He opened it and pulled out a scrap of cloth, holding it up for Eliza to see. "We found this snagged on a nail inside one of the hidden passageways at the museum. It appears to be part of a cleaning cloth."

Eliza's gaze fixed on the scrap of fabric. Her hands trembled slightly in her lap.

"And that's not all," Watson continued, reaching into the box once more. "Holmes and I discovered a hidden compartment in the lower part of that passageway. When we looked inside, we found this notebook along with some wires and a pulley system." He pulled out a small, leather-bound notebook, its cover worn and tattered.

Holmes said, "The notebook contains detailed descriptions of tricks, complete with drawings and instructions. Tricks that a magician might use to create illusions. Or someone who wanted to create eerie effects in a museum. We have checked the handwriting in the notebook. It matches the handwriting on your employee records, which we found in Mr Chamberlain's office."

A single tear rolled down Eliza's cheek, leaving a glistening trail on her skin. She bowed her head, her shoulders shaking with silent sobs.

Watson's expression softened, his brow furrowed with concern. "Why did you do it, Mrs Morton?" he asked.

Eliza sobbed quietly.

Holmes said softly, "You're in love with Marcus Bramwell, aren't you, Mrs Morton? You wanted to prove your love to him, to show him how much you cared."

More tears spilled down Eliza's cheeks. Her voice was barely audible as she spoke. "You're right, Mr Holmes. I do love Marcus, with all my heart."

Holmes nodded, his expression sympathetic. "You loved seeing how happy he was after hearing about the rumours of hauntings at the museum and how it was affecting Mr Chamberlain's business. It filled your heart with pride, knowing that you had made him so happy."

Eliza looked up, her eyes shining with tears. "Yes, it did. I wanted nothing more than to see him smile, to know that I had brought him joy."

"And the ultimate goal," Holmes continued, "was to close the museum, so that Marcus could buy it. You planned to tell him what you had done for him one day, to show him the depth of your love."

A sob escaped Eliza's lips, and she buried her face in her hands. Her shoulders shook as she wept.

Holmes and Watson exchanged a glance, their expressions a mix of sympathy and concern. Holmes knew that Eliza's actions, though misguided, had been driven by love. But he also knew that the consequences of her choices would be severe.

Eliza stopped crying. She looked up at Holmes and Watson. "I had to keep going with the illusions," she said, her voice trembling. "Seeing how happy they made Marcus, it was like a drug. I couldn't stop, even when I knew it was wrong."

Holmes said, "You didn't mean to hurt anyone, did you, Mrs Morton?"

Eliza shook her head vehemently. "No, of course not! I never wanted to cause any harm. And I certainly didn't mean to fool you and Dr Watson. I have the greatest respect for you both, truly I do."

Watson said, "But you did lie to us, Mrs Morton. About the things that had happened in the museum, about what people had said and things that had happened. To make us believe things were even worse. And, it threw the blame completely off you."

A flush of shame crept up Eliza's neck, staining her cheeks. "Yes, I did lie. And I'm so sorry for that. I never thought Mr Chamberlain would engage you. When I saw you there in the museum, I was so shocked, so afraid of being found out."

Holmes said, "We never had you down as a suspect, which is our fault and we should have known better. But, I must admit, you were extremely convincing, Mrs Morton. Can I ask, did Madam Rosalind actually give you a message from your late husband?"

Fresh tears came to Eliza's eyes. "She didn't. I'm so ashamed of bringing my Charlie into this mess. I don't recognise the woman I've become; a woman who so easily lies. But I couldn't stop myself. Oh, I know there could never be anything serious between Marcus and me; he has far younger woman fawning over him all the time. But it's the way he looks at me. No one ever looks at me like that. Not since my husband died."

Holmes smiled. "Everyone likes to be noticed, Mrs Morton. And people make mistakes where it comes to matters of the heart. Many a crime has been committed because of love."

"Including mine," Eliza said sadly. "What will happen now, Mr Holmes? I can't let Mr Chamberlain stay in prison."

Holmes said, "We will take you down to the police station, Mrs Morton. There, you can confess to your actions. I'm afraid you'll have to face the consequences."

Eliza's face crumpled, tears spilling down her cheeks. "I'm so scared, Mr Holmes. I don't know what will happen to me."

To her surprise, Holmes reached out and placed a hand on her shoulder, his touch gentle and reassuring. "I will stay by your side, Mrs Morton. I will make sure that you are treated fairly."

Eliza looked up at him, her eyes wide with disbelief. "You would do that for me? After everything I've done?"

Holmes' expression softened. "Much stronger crimes have been committed because of love, Mrs Morton. I understand the power it can hold over a person. And maybe, once Queen Victoria hears about your reasons for damaging her waxwork, she may offer some compassion towards you. After all, she is no stranger to love."

Eliza's shoulders shook with silent sobs, her head bowed in gratitude. "Thank you," she whispered, her voice choked with emotion. "Thank you both so much. I hope that one day, you can find it in your hearts to forgive me. I hope Mr Chamberlain will, too."

# Chapter 25

Later that day, Holmes and Watson returned to their home and settled down in their armchairs.

"Well!" Watson exclaimed. "You pulled in a lot of favours with the police today, Holmes. I do hope that leads to Mrs Morton receiving a softer sentence. That poor woman, falling for a man like Marcus Bramwell. I didn't dare tell her how dismissive he'd been about her when we spoke to him. How he laughed at how much she fawned over him. He's a truly obnoxious man. Not worth the likes of Mrs Morton whatsoever."

"I agree, Watson," Holmes said. "But people like Marcus Bramwell often end up receiving the treatment they dole out."

Dr Watson smiled, "Speaking of which, do you intend to talk to Madam Rosalind about those things she said at the séance?"

"About scores to be settled, and secrets deep within the walls? No, I've decided against it. Those claims could apply to any old building, and looking back, it was a generic thing for her to say. She probably says that at all places she visits. Also, I don't wish to give her the satisfaction of giving any credit to her words. I am content with never seeing that woman again."

"However," Dr Watson said, "I can sense there's something else you wish to say.

Holmes smiled. "You know me so well, my friend. Yes, I am content with never seeing that woman again. However, I have a feeling our paths will cross again soon. But for now, let's put all thoughts of Madam Rosalind to one side. Let us take a well-deserved rest, as I am sure we will soon be investigating a new mystery."

"One more thing before we put this behind us," Watson said. "Would you ever consider having a waxwork figure of yourself made? To display in some museum?"

Holmes laughed. "Not after this case! Anyway, I'd rather be immortalised in the written word, rather than wax. Mrs Morton was right about you, my dear friend, and how you have a way with words. And your stories, well, they will keep us alive for many years to come."

# A note from the author

For as long as I can remember, I have loved reading mystery books. It started with Enid Blyton's Famous Five, and The Secret Seven. As I got older, I progressed to Agatha Christie books, and of course, Sir Arthur Conan Doyle's Sherlock Holmes.

I love the characters of Sherlock Holmes and Dr Watson, and the Victorian era that the stories are set in. It seemed only natural that one day, I would write some of my own Sherlock stories. I love creating new mysteries for Mr Holmes, and his trusty companion, Dr John Watson. It's not just the era itself that seems to ignite ideas within me; it's also the characters who were around at that time, and the lives they led.

This story has been checked for errors, but if you see anything we have missed and you'd like to let us know about them, please email mabel@mabelswift.com

You can hear about my new releases by signing up to my newsletter www.mabelswift.com As a thank you for subscribing, I will send you a free short story: Sherlock Holmes and The Curious Clock.

If you'd like to contact me, you can get in touch via mabel@mabelswift.com I'd be delighted to hear from you.

Best wishes

Mabel